Also by Pagan Kennedy

Pagan Kennedy's Living:
The Handbook for Maturing Hipsters

'Zine: How I Spent Six Years of My Life in the Underground
and Finally Found Myself . . . I Think

Spinsters

Stripping and Other Stories

Platforms: A Microwaved Cultural Chronicle of the 1970s

The Exes

Pagan Kennedy

SCRIBNER PAPERBACK FICTION
Published by Simon & Schuster

SCRIBNER PAPERBACK FICTION
Simon & Schuster Inc.
Rockefeller Center
1230 Avenue of the Americas
New York, NY 10020

First Scribner Paperback Fiction edition 1999
SCRIBNER PAPERBACK FICTION and design are trademarks of
Jossey-Bass, Inc., used under license by
Simon & Schuster, the publisher of this work.

Manufactured in the United States of America

1 3 5 7 9 10 8 6 4 2

The Library of Congress has cataloged the
Simon & Schuster edition as follows:
Kennedy, Pagan.
The exes / Pagan Kennedy.
p. cm.
I. Title.
PS3561.E4269E95   1998
813'.54—dc21   97-47248
CIP

ISBN 0-684-83481-2
0-684-85442-2 (Pbk)

Acknowledgments

Thanks to my think tank, Humair Yusuf and Robby Virus. Both contributed lavishly of their time and expertise. The writing sisterhood—Nadine Boughton, Mary Clark, Karen Propp, and Lauren Slater—supplied the enthusiasm and detox tea that fueled this project. Laureen Connelly Rowland plucked me from the pages of *Wired* and brought me to Simon & Schuster; I'm grateful that she has remained a mentor and friend, even after her move to another house. And finally, thanks to Sarah Baker, who edited this manuscript so deftly.

The Exes

Contents

Hank

He used to wake up to the grit of Lilly's never-washed sheets, the smell of stale cigarettes, her clunky rings that fell off in the night and always ended up underneath him. It wasn't just the rings. Lilly's bed had been full of sharp objects. He'd wake up with a stabbing pain in his side and find that he'd been sleeping on a plastic army man or a barrette or a pencil stub or a Lucite ring.

Whatever it was, it would leave a weird set of wrinkles on his skin. In the beginning he had loved this, the way her bed branded him. After their first night together, he had tumbled out of her futon, pulled on his clothes and run to work because he was late; once he made it to the record store—chest still heaving from the sprint down Mass. Ave.—he'd lifted his shirt to show his coworkers the damage.

"Jesus," Sean had said, touching the marks. "What did she do to you, man?"

"It's her bed," Hank had explained, glowing with that new-relationship optimism. "Her bed is like the five-cent box at the Salvation Army. You wouldn't believe it. She does all her projects while she's lying under the covers. She's got everything in there—glue stick, scissors, toys."

In those first weeks, he meditated on Lilly all day long. As he stood behind the cash register, he would keep pretending to scratch his nose; this was so he could continually get whiffs of her pussy. He never washed the smell of her off his fingers if he could help it. And those marks that her bed left on his skin—the wrinkles, the indentations—he almost wished they would last forever, instead of fading away entirely, his skin turning flat and blank again, as if nothing had ever happened.

Many months later, though, he was just as glad that the marks disappeared without a trace. He already felt bruised enough by Lilly herself, never mind the bruises from her bed. Yeah, sure, it was great when she was in a good mood. He got sucked into her caffeine-buzzed, mind-meld, infatuation thing; but when she started acting crazed, then he turned crazed, too. He'd want to leave right in the middle of one of their fights, and she'd start crying as he walked out, and then he'd stew at work all day feeling alternately guilty and furious. When they were apart for long enough—a weekend, say—he'd turn back into his steady self again, just cruising along without any sudden stops or turns. That comforted him, the way it comforted him that the marks from her bed always disappeared so quickly from his skin; no matter what kind of madness he entered into with Lilly, his body always stayed its own smooth self.

"I'm a human Etch-A-Sketch," he would tell himself

sometimes. And that was a comforting thought, too. Lilly had an Etch-A-Sketch pad and she'd expertly twirl the dials to draw daisies, spirals, eyes, bodies; but when you shook the Etch-A-Sketch, her designs disappeared and the screen melted into its own gray blankness. He liked to think he only had to shake himself to clear away all the crap, the designs she kept trying to draw into him.

But there was only so much he could shake away. He came into work after hours of chasing Lilly through the streets, exhausted. Where once he'd stood in front of the cash register sniffing the pussy on his fingers, now he was just trying to keep it together enough to punch in the right numbers.

Sean had shaken his head when he heard. "That girl's a lunatic," he'd said. "Man, you've got to cut her loose. Her mood ring's gone permanently black, you know what I mean?"

And it was true: something was seriously wrong with Lilly, something that couldn't be cured by cigarettes or megavitamins or valerian tea. She had this disease that basically came down to her needing to be the center of attention at all times. She wore boas and striped stockings, platform shoes and a long ski hat that hung like a tail from her head; her voice sounded on the edge of hysteria, and you never knew when she was going to burst out laughing or burst into tears, insult you in front of your friends, crash your bike into a telephone pole, or yell at a cop. This was not all bad. In fact it was what attracted him in the beginning. She had so much white-trash poetry about her, the wildness of Elvis and Jerry Lee Lewis and Wanda Jackson all rolled into one. She made his heart bang like a rockabilly drumbeat.

When he was still in high school, he heard an obscure sixties song called "The Green Fuz" for the first time— somebody played it for him on a falling-apart stereo. The song sounded like it had been recorded in a basement on moldy tapes; you could just make out the furry sounds of the guitar chomping down on the melody, and the singer growling, "Come along, baby, and see where we go. We're the Green Fuz." That was it, the original garage-band sound, the first American punk rock, a primitive blast of outrage that sat like a heap of steaming dung on top of the minty-fresh wasteland of his suburban teenage life. Once he heard "The Green Fuz," he understood that guys like him—guys with Ivory Soap skin and a drizzle of blond hair, guys from the Midwest who'd been Eagle Scouts—guys like him could be raw, too. And right at that moment he began aching to make that kind of music, an ache that had never left him since.

The first time he saw Lilly, she was pogoing center stage at the Rat, her dreadlocks flying. He'd threaded his way through the crowd until he stood behind her so he could watch how she slitted her eyes as she bumped against the people around her. Her face was so shiny—at first he thought she was drenched in sweat, and then he realized that she was crying.

"Don't cry," he said. Actually he'd had to yell it into her ear. And then she'd opened her eyes, put her arms around him, and they'd sort of slow-danced. Corny as it sounds, this all seemed perfectly natural at the time. More than natural. It seemed as if they were following a script.

And maybe it was part of the script, too, that their whole girlfriend-boyfriend thing would last only a year. It ended after the eight-track incident, as they later called it. They'd been standing in his room screaming at each other about something—he couldn't even remember what afterward—and Lilly had reached out a steel-tipped combat-booted toe and stepped on one of his eight-track tapes. She broke it with a twisting motion of her ankle, as if she were stubbing out a cigarette.

"Oh my God," he said, dropping down on his hands and knees to examine the shards. "This is Kiss's *Love Gun*. Do you know how many yard sales I went to before I found this?"

"Is that all you can say? You care more about your stupid tapes than me."

"You bet I do," he said, standing up and leaning near her, straining toward some awful moment.

"Well, fuck you," she yelled. And then she pushed over a pile of eight-tracks and began stomping on them, throwing them around until his room was hung with black streamers of tape and bits of the plastic cases.

None of their fights had ever before led to the destruction of rare musical media—that was the thought that kept running through his mind. It seemed like they'd crossed some line together. He had stood absolutely still as she threw the tapes around, barely flinching when one of them hit his face. He'd felt like a slow-motion man stuck in the middle of a fast-motion film—immobilized with anger, all his muscles tensed. He thought that if he moved at all, he would punch her, slam her against the wall, stick one of those tape shards into her eye.

And then, while he was still stuck there, she had stormed out and left him in the sudden silence of a room draped in black bunting. He knew then how deep the marks went, those wrinkled marks of daily hurt and insult. They wriggled all over his skin; they burrowed into his brain. He stumbled into the bathroom and leaned over the toilet. He thought he was going to puke, but nothing came out.

After the eight-track incident, they'd avoided each other for a week or so. Finally, they'd met at a diner to hash it all out. When Lilly slid into the booth opposite him, he sensed something between them had changed. She was oddly lucid and calm that night; so was he. Their madness together seemed to have broken like a fever.

There were certain meals with girlfriends he'd always remember, like the lime-and-peanut-flavored noodles he and Deb ate before they kissed that first time, lips still burning with spice; or the dripping containers of Chinese food that he and Kelly had once wolfed down as they sat out on her roof. With other women those important meals—meals that felt like perfect moments of understanding—came at the beginning of relationships. But with Lilly, the important meal came at the end.

They sat in Dell's Diner and ordered a piece of pecan pie with two forks. But when the pie came, they hadn't used the forks; instead, they'd taken turns picking pecans off the top of the pie. They'd eaten entirely with their hands, leaving a slick of yellow-goo pie filling untouched on the plate. He remembered watching her fingers, how her rings flashed with each delicate movement.

"Why are we so mean?" she'd asked him. "How does it start? I never notice it starting. It's like we're little kids who don't know how to play nicely together. We need some adult to come along and tell us to behave."

"I know," he said. "We always get so hysterical around each other." He meant that she got hysterical, but he didn't want to say that.

"So what are we going to do?"

"Well," he said, chewing reflectively on a pecan. "I guess we're going to have to figure out how to get along better."

"What if the only way is to break up?" she said. "I've been thinking that's maybe the only way. Were you thinking that?"

"No, but that makes perfect sense," he said. "God, that really depresses me."

"Actually, it might not be all that bad." She lit a cigarette and then passed it to him, as if they were inmates in the same cell. "I've already thought about it. I had this idea that we could be something else besides boyfriend and girlfriend."

"What do you mean? You mean like 'Let's just be friends'? Please, Lilly, don't start."

"No, no, no," she said, leaning forward.

"Well, what?"

"We could play music together." He remembered how she said that, looking straight at him with her gold eyes. Later he thought that maybe the moment he and Lilly broke up, they also fell in love. Not romantic love, but a new kind of love he didn't know the name for. Maybe he'd always been attracted to her as an artist; maybe their sexual relationship had been a rehearsal for some deeper connection.

Looking back years later, he realized how he'd been preparing her. When they met, she could pick out a few measly chords on her guitar; by the time they broke up, she could play anything from *Led Zeppelin III*. He'd spent a lot of time jamming with her, had helped her install a whammy bar on her Gibson and given her a bunch of effects boxes.

While they were sleeping together, they hadn't been able to jam together without ending up in a fight. He'd find himself nit-picking, always turning into her teacher. "Lilly, that bar chord is sloppy. Try to hold on tighter," he'd hear himself say, regretting it even as it came out of his mouth.

A comment like that could reduce her to tears. "I *can't*. I can't do it just the way you do, Hank," she would say. But all the while she was learning so fast it frightened him. He'd been noodling on his guitar since he was a kid, and here she was keeping up with him, improvising little melody lines as he played chord changes for her. He hated the idea that someday he might not have anything left to teach her.

Back then, back when they were sleeping together, she'd

come up with ideas for songs and he'd almost always shoot them down. Months after they broke up, though, her ideas haunted him like the ghosts of songs, like tunes you half remember and can't get out of your head. She'd wanted, for instance, to tie a walkie-talkie to a microphone and sing to it from another walkie-talkie; she would be standing in another room—maybe outside the house entirely—as he accompanied the walkie-talkie with his guitar. At the time, he thought she'd come up with this idea just to be a pain in the butt. "The reason people play in the same room is so that they *hear each other,*" he'd growled. "Call me an old fuddy-duddy, but I think that's important."

"Forget it. Just forget it," she'd said, and stormed out.

But months after they'd split, his instinct for what would make good music began to kick in again. He had to admit the walkie-talkie thing might have worked. It would have been a great gimmick on stage, anyway. One thing was for sure: it was better than any of the lame ideas his bandmates had come up with. He'd been in plenty of bands over the years—bands that got mediocre reviews in grotty little fanzines; bands that posed together on the boardwalk, with Sonic Youth scowls on their faces; guitar-hero bands where everyone tried to drown each other out. He recognized in Lilly something that none of those pouting guys had— something he didn't have himself.

So he'd called her and asked if she really wanted to be in a band with him. By this time, she'd fallen in love with some art fag, and he was going out with his upstairs neighbor, so the sexual thing was no longer an issue. "Sure I want to be

in a band, Hank," she said over the phone. "I knew you'd
come crawling back to me eventually." And then she'd
laughed her just-this-side-of-hysteria laugh.

When they got together to practice that first time, she'd
sat on her bed and he'd settled on a pile of dirty laundry on
the opposite side of the room. They'd been ultrapolite.

"Maybe you should speed that up a little," he'd heard
himself say.

"Okay. Like this?" she would say, and try different kinds
of riffs until he nodded.

And suddenly there was this good thing between them.
It reminded him of one of his favorite tasks at work—giving the guys in the warehouse instructions over the phone.
Hank, who'd worked at the store for years, knew every inch
of that warehouse. But the warehouse guys came and
went—they got promoted, or quit, or only worked during
the summer—so when they needed to find something
they'd call him up. "Yo, man," they'd say. "We got some orders for Nancy Sinatra. We can find Frank but no Nancy."

"Okay, you see that stack of wooden crates?" he'd say.

"Um, wait a sec, okay, yeah."

"Now walk to your right." Hank would keep giving
careful directions, moving the guy all around the warehouse until he was standing in just the right spot. Sometimes Hank would feel this incredible oneness with the
person on the other end—the guy who was letting Hank
move his body around the warehouse, turn his head, look
through his eyes. That was the kind of oneness he felt with
Lilly now. Together they were exploring this vast, dark

warehouse full of music. He knew the way around, but she was the one who could see and feel; she was the one who could reach up and grasp what glimmered in the half-light on the highest shelf.

"Why don't you work on some of your songs?" Hank told her after their first session. Making up songs was never a problem for Lilly. The next time they practiced, she began strumming her guitar and singing in the earnest, breathy way of a kid chanting a nursery rhyme: "If you peel off my Band-Aid do it quick, because it only hurts when you let it stick." The whole song was about Band-Aids; it sounded like a lullaby your dead aunt would sing to you in a dream.

A few days later, Lilly had called with that hysterical pitch in her voice. "I have to talk to you right now," she'd said. "I know what our band should be named. Okay, okay, you ready? We'll call ourselves the Exes. And the thing is, we will be exes—everyone in the band will have gone out with someone else in the band."

"What?" He'd forgotten how intense Lilly could get. "We've only practiced twice. Let's not name this thing until we're sure it's going to work."

"No, no, I've figured it all out," she said. He could imagine her pacing around her room, smoking so furiously that she lit a new cigarette even before she stubbed out the old one.

"What did you say? The Exes? Everyone will get us confused with X. They'll think we're trying to be an X cover band."

"No," Lilly said impatiently. "I already thought of that.

For one thing, X is broken up, so they're not around any-way. And on top of that, we'll have the gossip factor. Like, okay, everyone will hear about us and they'll say, 'That band is made up entirely of exes? Well, who went out with who? And how do they all get along now?' I'm telling you, Hank, people are going to go nuts trying to figure out how ex-boyfriends and -girlfriends can stand to be around each other enough to be in a band—that will make us instantly intriguing."

Back when he was sleeping with Lilly, he would have said, "Forget it. This is crazy." But as her bandmate, he could see her idea had a certain genius. "So what about the other band members," he said. "I mean, do we have to sleep with them? What if the only drummer we can get is Roddy—are you willing to do that for art?"

"No, silly. We can't sleep with someone just to get them in the band. That's cheating. We have to find people we've already gone out with. Or people who've gone out with each other."

Neither of them could think of any other exes that they wanted to be in a band with. "I guess we'll just have to find an ex-couple. What we really need is a bassist and a drum-mer," Hank said. "A bass player and a drummer who went out with each other, broke up, and now get along fine. That's not going to be easy."

But once he started asking around, he realized how inces-tuous the rock world was. All you had to do was locate the women rockers: every one of them had a whole constella-tion of musician exes.

The one he wanted was Shazia Dohra, the bassist for Sluggo. She had great chops, and best of all, he'd heard that she'd slept with lots of rockers around town, male and female. That would make things easy.

The trouble was, how would he ever convince her to join the Exes? Her band had signed a deal with Bronco Records, the largest indie label in the country. Why would she drop out of Sluggo so she could join a band that didn't even exist yet? There was hope. According to *The Sound*—a gossip sheet for Boston bands—the members of Sluggo hated each other's guts.

When you followed *The Sound* regularly, you began to believe that the only real scene flourished inside the Middle East, T.T.'s, the Paradise, and Dell's Diner. The borders of *The Sound*'s rock 'n' roll landscape ended at the shores of the Boston Harbor and at the Newton line where WZBC broadcast and along the hazy border where Somerville turned into Charlestown; beyond this charted territory, all was blank and hazy, a land of mists. *The Sound* reported on a fiercely local tribe, suspicious of outsiders. The smeared-newsprint pages bristled with a secret language of gossip, in-jokes, and references to obscure bands and personages.

When Hank first moved to Boston, he couldn't understand most of what he read in *The Sound;* a few years later, he himself had become an in-joke. One day, flipping through the gossip column, he saw his own name in boldface and his stomach hurt even before he read the item: "We hear **Hank Alvey** got booted out of the Ancient Astronauts because of his 'artistic differences' with everyone else. Now he's joined the Thrifties, and word has it that he's trying to tell them what to do, too. No wonder Hank has been called the Ross Perot of the Boston music scene."

Hank felt sick when he read that. "They got it all wrong," he'd said to Sean. "I didn't get kicked out of the Ancient Astronauts. Oh man, do people really think I'm like Ross Perot? Does everyone say that behind my back?"

"Don't worry," Sean had said. "*The Sound* slags everybody at least once. It's like a rite of passage."

But it hadn't been just once. For a few months, he'd become a running joke in the gossip column. "Sources tell us that **Petey Marcos** will be starting a band called Kleenex Jr.," he read one day, glimpsing with dread his own name hovering in the next sentence. "Which reminds us of **Hank Alvey**. We here at *The Sound* have noticed that Hank goes through bands as if they're certain tissue products." He'd become so paranoid about his reputation that after the Thrifties broke up, he hadn't joined another band. The whole time he and Lilly were together, he'd only played in his room.

Maybe it was true that he'd gone through bands as if they were Kleenex: He had good reason to. He kept ending up with these guys who could play perfectly well, but who just didn't have *it,* whatever *it* was. Hank didn't have it either, but at least he could recognize the people who did. He knew Shazia Dohra had it, the way she slid her fingers around the bass, making funky little hiccups of sound, and thrust her hips out with every beat. She wore a skintight T-shirt that said GIRLS KICK ASS and black jeans that had gotten greasy with age; she had big tits but somehow managed to seem androgynous anyway, with her short hair and Johnny Thunders scowl.

Why should she leave Sluggo, those four guys standing around her in their sideburns and Converse All-Stars and goatees like some kind of slacker harem?

Hank decided to take his time. Stealing Shazia would be like stealing someone's girlfriend. The trick is to hang around, act friendly, encourage her to confide in you, and then pounce. This was the strategy he would use to get Shazia.

After one of their shows, he came up to her and said, "That was great, really great. But I wish I could have heard your bass better. They should turn you up."

She probably thought he was trying to hit on her. "Yeah, well, thanks," she said noncommittally. "You know how it is. But thanks."

And then one day she meandered into the record store, ran her hand along the LPs, paused before the New Wave section, and finally came up and asked him for the key to the case full of used CDs. A few minutes later, she returned to the register with a Black Girls CD.

"Hey," he said, "so what's Sluggo up to lately? You know I'm a big fan."

She craned her neck so she could meet his eyes—he towered over people when he stood on the platform behind the register. "Um," she said, drawing out the single syllable as if she were trying to make some kind of decision about him.

"Well, we're talking about touring, but it's hard to agree when you've got five people. Actually, the whole thing is kind of fucked-up right now." Her voice cracked.

Hank made a sympathetic noise in his throat, hoping she'd spill the story.

Instead, her eyes skittered away from his. "I should go," she said. She looked miserable.

He began punching in the price of her CD, and then held it up a minute. "I really like this album—I like bands with women in them. They're usually a lot more interesting."

"Yeah right," Shazia said, laughing warily. "Every band needs a pair of tits, right? That's how you get ahead in this business."

"Look, no, you know I didn't mean anything like that." Hank shifted his eyes all around, suddenly finding no safe place for them to settle. He was paranoid that he'd been staring at her tits the whole time they were talking. Even now, he could just see them at the lower fringes of his vision, where they strained against the fabric of her T-shirt. He dragged his gaze to the top of her head. "I mean"— Hank cleared his throat—"it's just that women are more original. They haven't been through the whole guy-rock assembly line, you know?"

"Yeah. I'm sorry. I didn't mean to get all feminist on you."

"Listen," he said. "Um, I'm just starting this band with a woman guitarist. She writes all the songs. If you'd like to come by sometime, you could hear our stuff, maybe jam with us . . . " His hands were sweating as he put her CD into a bag and he didn't dare look up.

She shrugged. "Okay, maybe."

He waited until she walked out of the store, and then rubbed his face. "Goddamn. What was all that about?" he thought. Watching Shazia on stage, he'd assumed she was one of those inarticulate, drop-dead-cool people whose secret weapon is their aloofness—no matter how much you need them, they'll never need you. And in a way, she was that. But for a moment, he'd seen right into her, and what he'd seen was himself. Or rather, he'd seen the Hank of eight months ago, the guy who staggered around in between those fights with Lilly—a sleep-deprived, half-mad zombie pretending to be a human being. He could tell Shaz was going through some kind of hell.

A few weeks later, she called. "Do you still want me to come by and play with you guys?" she said. Her voice had regained that tuff-girl flatness, like she could take him or leave him. "Where's the practice space?"

Hank rattled off the address. He and Lilly had started renting the space several months ago—a dank room in the basement of a junk shop. They would sit among the piles of *Life* magazine, the mothball-smelling clothes, the heads and hands of mannequins, Lilly with her guitar on one knee, Hank with his keyboard on his lap.

The two of them shared a secret world down there in the basement; the place had taken on the atmosphere of a kids' clubhouse. They even had an imaginary friend, because Lilly had named the drum machine Ivan. "Tell Ivan to shut up," she'd say. "God, he is such a cheeseball." Ivan became, in their minds, the ultimate rock 'n' roll loser, an over-thehill heavy metal guy who lived in some shag-carpeted apartment and worked as a cashier at Star Market.

They'd even made up their own secret handshake: You held your fingers into a Vulcan "live long and prosper" V, and then you slid your V into the V of the other person's hand, to form a sort of three-dimensional X. "Give me the shake, the X shake," Lilly would say to Hank whenever they worked out some difficult part in a song. They'd shake and then slap five. "We rule," she'd yell.

But it was even more twisted than that. Down in the basement late at night—the world gone silent outside, the blue-white beam of a streetlight falling through their one window—they had begun pretending that the Exes already existed as a band, the kind that headlined at Lollapalooza and made rock videos.

"This might be a good dress to wear when I'm on the cover of *Spin,*" Lilly would say, holding up a polyester prom gown that she'd found on the pile of old clothes. "Don't you think?"

"Too frumpy," Hank would tell her. "The miniskirt-and-combat-boot thing is better. You know, the *vagina dentata* look."

"*Vagina dentata!* That'll be the name of our first album. Or maybe the second album." And so it would go, the two of them plotting the arc of their legendary career.

Back when he and Lilly slept together, he'd refused to encourage her in this way. Her wild imagination—her delusions of grandeur, really—had annoyed the hell out of him. Sitting in a club, she could become convinced that the people at the next table were staring at her; once she yelled at her housemate for copying the way she dressed. Hank would find himself running around apologizing to everyone, patching things up, saying, "Look, you know she didn't mean it. She gets carried away sometimes." But now he almost never saw Lilly in the outside world anymore, and down here in the basement, it didn't matter how she acted. So he let himself fantasize right along with her; while they practiced, he too posed for the imaginary cameras of a rock-video producer, twisting his whammy bar like he was Jimmy Page or something. He imagined fame bearing down on him like a tour bus that someday would stop beside him and open its hinged doors to a lavish interior, so that he could climb up and recline on a plush seat. Down in the practice room, he never doubted fame would arrive like that, right on schedule, to whisk him away.

He wasn't sure what would happen if someone else entered the fantasy world of the basement. He could snap back into reality, but could Lilly?

"Listen, I'll do the talking," he said to her the night Shazia was supposed to show. "You know how you can freak people out sometimes. And don't mention the exboyfriend, ex-girlfriend thing. She's not ready for that yet."

"Geez, you don't need to treat me like a retard," Lilly said, pulling her guitar strap off. "Do you have a crush on this girl or something?"

He could hear the annoyance creeping into her voice and was afraid this might be their first fight as bandmates. "You think I want another girlfriend? I've already got my hands full with Deb," he said, referring to the upstairs neighbor who'd begun sleeping in his bed. "It's just—Shazia's the only bassist I can imagine us having."

"You've got a musical crush on her," Lilly said, fishing her cigarettes out of her purse.

"Yeah, I guess so."

"But you have a bigger musical crush on me, right?"

"Yeah," he said, laughing, glad the fight had been averted. "I think you're an unrecognized genius that I'm the first to recognize. Which makes me a genius too."

Later, when Shazia knocked on the door—and he led her through the maze of boxes saying, "Sorry, it's kind of a mess down here," and cleared a seat for her—Lilly did keep quiet. She gazed at Shazia through her dreadlocks and said, "Hey," and then went back to fiddling with her guitar. At that moment, Hank realized he could trust Lilly, really trust her to keep herself glued together when she had to.

"Why don't we play some of our songs, and you can just start jamming with us when you're ready," he said to Shazia after he'd gotten her amped in. "Let's do that Band-Aid song, Lill."

They played it through a couple of times, Shazia adding in a bell-like, Elvis-Sun sessions bass line.

"Wait a sec, I've got an idea. Here, Lill, you just sing," he said. "I'll take the guitar part." And he played in this twangy, banjo-y way; and they all readjusted until the song mutated from a nursery rhyme into a honky-tonk stomp. All night was like that—they barely had to speak as they turned songs inside out. He hadn't noticed before that, original as they were, all of Lilly's songs sounded the same—too much the product of an unhinged art-school girl who couldn't really play her guitar. "This one's got too much clove cigarette in it," he'd say. "Let's give it more malt liquor. More Isaac Hayes." And Shazia would—she could do funk, soul, power pop, country, whatever.

It all went great until Shazia flipped her wrist to look at her watch and said, "I've got to go, you guys."

"Listen, I hope you'll come back," Hank said, trying to play it cool.

"Yeah, sure." She turned those black eyes on him and he couldn't tell what she was thinking. But then, as she left, she paused in front of Lilly. "Write down your phone number for me, will you?" she said.

Hank broke out in a sweat. It was turning into one of those nightmares where the worst and most obvious thing happens. Chicks bonding. He saw it all coming. Shazia would steal Lilly away, form an all-girl band, make it big, and one day he'd pick up *Forced Exposure* and read an interview where they referred to him as the loser guy who'd introduced them.

For days after, he had an urge to bike over to Lilly's house and demand to know what was going on. But instead he waited until their Monday-night practice session before he confronted her. "So, um, Lill, did she call?"

"Who?" Lilly said, dumping her stuff and settling into a pile of clothes.

"Shazia," he said sullenly. "She took your number, remember?"

"Oh yeah." Lilly began unpacking her guitar. "No, she didn't call because I saw her at the Valkyries show. She said you treat me like a trained monkey. I guess she wanted to awake my feministical awareness or something. I told her I needed to be treated like a trained monkey or else I start acting like an untrained monkey."

"Oh geez." Hank put his head in his hands. "What else did she say?"

"'Cool.' She said, 'That's cool.' I started dancing with her. We were slamming against everyone else. And I got really drunk and told her about the Exes. Don't be mad, Hank. She thought it was funny."

Hank was never sure exactly what went on between the two of them, but he didn't ask. They had some chick thing going that he didn't want to tamper with. Because that night, Shazia knocked at their practice-room door, and after that she often drifted in with her long, black guitar case. She didn't so much join the band as insinuate herself into it. She reminded Hank of the stray cat who had once begun meowing at his door, who scurried in to eat a bowl of food but would disappear for days and never quite became a pet.

With Shazia—or Shaz as she called herself—they settled into a new routine. They became all business now, working out little riffs and bridges, and even inventing new instruments when they had to. Lilly bought some Fisher-Price walkie-talkies at a thrift store and Hank rigged them up to an amp and a set of effects boxes, so they could finally do the walkie-talkie song she'd thought up more than a year ago.

Shaz worked by instinct. She cultivated mystery. "We can't call this song 'Dee Cee,'" she said once. "It's bad luck." But when he questioned her, she wouldn't explain. "It's only a feeling," she said, giving the impression that just the opposite was true, that something had happened to her in D.C. and she couldn't bear to talk about it.

Sometimes Hank wondered if Shazia was like that because of the faith thing. She'd grown up Muslim, which was probably like growing up Catholic or born-again Baptist—those hard-core religions tended to make people tempestuous and twisted in a way he envied. As a kid, whenever he'd asked his atheist parents a question, they'd resorted to a scientific explanation. Sex was just eggs and sperm. Death was just cells decaying. No wonder he had so little passion to put into his music now. What could he scream about on stage? What pain did he know? Nothing, unless you counted the death of his poodle Mittens. But at least he recognized passion when he heard it. At least he'd always had that.

Back in his old boyhood room, with its repeating pattern of football players on the wall and its clean smell of pine furniture, he used to crouch over the turntable to catch the scratchy singing of bluesmen, their voices as wrinkled as their faces, fingerprints of pain. He'd tune in on Sunday, searching the dial for gospel music. Sometimes he'd manage to find a station from some faraway place like Detroit. And though the signal was weak and crackling, those gospel singers reached out through the radio and squeezed his heart. Their voices cracked with love for Jesus and made him want to crack, too, crack himself wide open to something he didn't understand.

Lilly and Shaz both came from faraway places like the ones he heard on the radio, places where people still believed. Lilly's mother had dragged her through so many Holy Rollers' tents that she could still sing all the Pentecostal hymns by heart. And Shaz, with her flat American accent and a Muslim family she never talked about—the atmosphere of tragedy wafted around her like musk.

Maybe that's why the two of them got along so well, he thought. Lilly never questioned Shaz's crazy whims. When Shaz refused to call that song "Dee Cee," Lilly said, "You're totally right. What was I thinking? D.C. is an unlucky city, with the five-sided Pentagon and everything."

Half the time he couldn't understand what the hell the two of them were talking about. "Is Shaz in our band?" he asked Lilly once.

"I don't know. You're the leader," she said.

"So you guys didn't talk about it? What do you talk about?"

"Oh, you know," Lilly said. "Stuff that annoys us. Or music we like. And of course"—she paused to take a drag on her cigarette—"your dick size. Oh, calm down, Hank, I'm only kidding. We have better things to talk about than your dick."

"Did you ever find out what's going on with her and Sluggo?"

"She's really pissed at those guys, but every time I try to ask about it, she gets all embarrassed. I'd say somebody in that band is psycho, but I don't know who."

Hank leaned forward. "Okay, but what about her joining us? Does she want to join?"

Lilly blew out a long stream of smoke. "You don't get it. I'm trying to figure out whether we want her, Hank. If she's so pissed at them, who's to say she won't get pissed at us? Maybe she's the psycho one."

Hank stared off at the weeping cement wall of their underground room; under the glare of the bare bulb, it reminded him of sweaty skin. Why didn't he ever think about stuff like that? He always assumed people were as plain and straight as he was. Why did everyone else have these dark folds, these wrinkles and kinks to them?

"Shit," he said.

"Actually," Lilly said, turning away from him to pack up her guitar, "I bet she's fine. She's just a lot different from us, is all."

"How's she different?" Hank wanted to know, but Lilly only shrugged.

A few days later, he picked up *The Sound* and glimpsed Shaz's name in the gossip column. "**Sluggo** is on their way to the big time—CD out soon and an upcoming European tour bankrolled by the big daddies at Bronco Records," the magazine said. "Frankly, we're amazed that Sluggo has gotten this far, considering the way those boys squabble. Temper, temper, temper. We hear that bassist **Shazia**

Dohra—the only chick in the band, we might add—is now officially an ex-member. We're dying to know: Did she jump or was she pushed?"

The next time Shaz came to practice, Hank waved *The Sound* in front of her. "Why didn't you tell me? You must be really pissed off."

Shaz bit her lip and looked at him sideways. "I hate this. I didn't want to make a big thing out of it, but now it's all around town."

"Can I ask what happened?"

Shaz glanced down, thinking. "I don't know how to explain it. I just . . . I have to have my own life. I couldn't go with them on that tour."

Hank felt his brow wrinkle. "You mean you quit? Oh my God. Do you know how many people would kill to go on a tour like that? And you didn't want to go?"

Shaz shrugged. "I'm not going to give up everything just so maybe I can be a rock star someday. I just think that's dumb."

"Oh," he said, nodding his head, as if he agreed. "Well, you're not exactly going to have that problem with us." He gestured around at the heaps of clothes, the musty magazines. "We don't have any tours in Europe planned for the near future."

"Yeah, that's why I like playing with you guys," she said, sitting down on top of an amp. "You guys have the right attitude."

Lilly glared at Hank. He knew what Lilly was thinking: You better set her straight.

Instead, Hank cleared his throat. "Well, um, do you think you might want to join us? Officially, I mean."

"Okay," Shaz said, opening her guitar case. "If you want me to. The only thing is, I come and go as I please. That has to be the deal."

"What do you say, Lill? Should we let her in?" he called. "Can you live with that deal?"

"You have to have an ex, you know," Lilly said. "Don't forget. Do you have an ex who's a drummer?"

Shaz laughed in that way she had—rolling her eyes and shaking her head at some ridiculous thought she was having. "Yeah, I've got someone for you."

A few days later, she showed up with this tall guy trailing behind her. He had thick black hair that hung in his eyes, his Adam's apple jutted from his skinny neck, and he wore sawed-off shorts with pen doodles all over them. He carried a high-hat cymbal on its stand, holding it aloft like some kind of torch. "Hey, how you doing?" he said. "I brought my drum kit in the van. Where should I put it?"

That really pissed Hank off—Shaz hadn't even warned him that this guy was coming, and now the guy himself just assumed he could move his drums in, as if he could join a band as easily as dropping by for a beer. But there was one reason Hank wanted this guy in the band immediately. The guy had said the magic word. The magic word was "van."

Hank bounded up the stairs and out onto the street; there it waited, double-parked and still rumbling. It was a shabbier and smaller version of the tour bus he'd once imagined bearing down on him, the tour bus that would one day whisk him off to the dry ice–hazy heaven of the rock 'n' roll big time.

For a minute, Hank stood on the sidewalk just staring, overjoyed. Shaz appeared beside him. "That's Walt," she said. "And that's his van."

He turned out to be your typical drummer—only worse. He could jump right into any song without a problem, but as soon as they stopped to fix one of Lilly's strings and tune up her guitar again, Walt got bored. Basically he couldn't sit still for more than five minutes. He jumped up and started drumming the walls, the mannequin heads, the boxes, the amps, drumming his way through the practice space and out the door. Presumably he would have drummed himself down the street if Shaz hadn't run out after him. "Walt, Walt." She laughed. "Come back here."

But as soon as they started playing, Walt became the perfect drummer—twirling his sticks high in the air and catching them at that last precarious moment before he needed them, asking Hank where to put the fills, lapsing into a sotto snare beat whenever Lilly sang, so as not to drown her out.

"Where did you get that guy?" Hank asked Shaz after the Waltmobile had driven away. "And how come he's not in a real band?"

"Walt? I've known him ever since I lived in San Francisco. The thing is, he doesn't get out much." She stood with her hands on her hips, staring at the drum set that now took up half their practice space. "I can't believe I'm in a band with Walt," she said, half to herself. Then she said to

Hank, "You can kick him out if he's too weird. I don't know, this may have been really stupid of me."

"Why?" He tried to keep his voice even. "What's wrong with him?"

Shaz turned to look at Hank. "Oh no, he's fine now, you know, but he checked himself into a mental hospital a while ago."

"Oh geez."

"No, it's okay." Shaz fixed him with that intensely sincere gaze of hers. "He's on Prozac now. He's really trying to straighten out his life and have more friends. He just quit grad school, too, which was really good . . ."

"Isn't that usually bad, dropping out of school?"

"Not for him. It was just making him worse. He's pretty together now. He's got a job at the post office."

"Oh, the post office. Yeah, he's in good hands now," Hank said, trying to make a joke. Shaz gazed back at him, confused—maybe she didn't get it. "Okay, whatever." Hank added, "Do you think he can handle being in a band?"

"Yeah, sure," she said.

"So," Hank said, eyeing the drum set that seemed to sprawl across the room like a huge animal, "we're kind of getting in on the ground floor here. Is that what you're saying? It's like we're getting him at the Salvation Army—you know, a real deal that nobody else has spotted yet because it's hidden behind other stuff. Is that how it is?" Hank was inclined to think the best.

"Yeah," Shaz said. "But just don't mention any of this to

him—you know, the Prozac or anything. And *don't* tell him that he's in here as my ex. I'll tell him, okay?"

While Shaz was explaining the Walt situation to him, Hank felt like it was dealable. But as soon as Hank climbed on his bike and peddled past Bunratty's—where the drunk punks poured out onto the sidewalk, talking and laughing about the show they'd just seen—Hank hit bottom. The Exes would never even play Bunratty's, he could feel it in his bones. Walt summed up everything wrong with the Exes; none of them could make it in the real world of bands. They were a lonely hearts club, a collection of psychotic losers. They'd be stuck in that basement for the rest of their lives, writing songs that were not called "Dee Cee" and taking their medication.

To top it off, when he walked into his room, he found Deb sitting on his bed, crying. "It's two in the morning," she said. "You're always at that stupid practice space. I wish it had a phone."

"What? What is it?" He sat next to her and held her. He didn't have it in him to argue.

"The restaurant's closing. I'm going to lose my job. I just wanted"—here she sobbed—"I just wanted to come home and have somebody give me a back rub. But you're never around. You know, I could have a normal boyfriend if I wanted to."

"Come on now, stop it," he said, stroking her hair. "You're really busy, too. You barely have any time for me."

"Yeah, but now I'm unemployed and I'm going to be alone and depressed all the time."

"No you won't," he said, trying to hide his dread. He could see how this relationship of convenience was turning into a real relationship. He and Deb had been sleeping with each other for six months now; he'd hoped they could keep treading water forever, treading like little kids in a pond, looking at each other over the black surface of the water and feeling the currents made by each other's bodies—not touching, not connecting, but floating nearby. Now he understood that, without meaning to, you always drifted closer and closer until finally you were batting and bumping the other person. In your struggle to stay afloat you lashed out. You hit and hurt.

"I've had an awful day too," he said. "Look. Let's just go to bed and deal with it all in the morning."

And he was right. The next day, none of it seemed so bad. "I hated that job anyway. What was I thinking?" Deb said. He watched her bike off toward school, feeling her safely distant again, autonomous.

And then, a few hours after Hank got to work, Walt dropped by wearing a mail carrier's outfit: crisp blue shorts, button-down shirt, pith helmet, the whole deal. Walt looked so reputable—so much like a representative of the U.S. Postal Service, with its schedules and routes, its precise scales and nine-digit zip codes—that Hank felt a new confidence in him.

"I remembered that you worked here, so I drove over on my break. I love driving around in the mail mobile," Walt said, pointing out the window at the white truck out front, parked halfway up on the curb and flashing its hazards.

"That's beautiful, man," Hank said reverently. It seemed to him that Walt was slightly magical, the way he always appeared with some oversized vehicle. "You're a representative of the U.S. government. You've got the insignia."

"Yeah, I try not to abuse my power. Listen, I just wanted to tell you that I scored a sixteen-track mixer from this friend of mine. I've got it in the truck out there."

"Can I see it?" Hank said, and they trotted outside and climbed inside the truck. There it sat between two mail bags—a monolith covered with knobs, levers, dangling wires. It looked like it had just been ripped out of some 1970s recording studio.

"Don't worry," Walt said. "I know how to hook it up." He was crammed in the truck beside Hank, stooping so he wouldn't hit his head on the low ceiling. Up close, Hank noticed how skinny Walt was and how he smelled of sweat and polyester.

"I hear you're a genius," Hank said, as he climbed back down onto the sidewalk. "Shaz said you used to be a biologist at Harvard."

Walt stared down at him. "I'm through with all that. I'm a normal guy now. I have the uniform." He gestured at the shorts that half covered his toothpick legs and the pith helmet that sat at a crazy angle on top of his Prince Valiant hair.

"Oh, okay," Hank said. "I'll keep that in mind."

Two nights later, Walt showed up at the practice space with an armload of recording equipment. He hunched in the corner, patching the wires together and talking to himself: "This can go here. And we can tape this to the floor . . ."

"Walt," Shaz scolded. "We're all waiting. Do that later." She and Hank had just naturally fallen into the role of keeping their respective exes under control.

Now, suddenly, Hank understood how this could work. They'd turned from four people into two couples—like Lucy and Ricky and Fred and Ethel. A vintage-sitcom dynamic was at work here: the couples bickered but never really fought; the girls hung out together and plotted against the guys; the guys bonded. For a moment, Hank had this whole, dizzying *I Love Lucy* vision of the band. He himself was Ricky, the professional one; and Lilly was Lucy, with her kooky schemes. Shaz and Walt would be like the Mertzes, popping in the door at the right moment, content with their role as supporting actors.

But it was more than that. The Exes had begun to sound tight, like a real band. Something huge and scary was at work. Hank felt like he was falling in love with the Exes. It seemed like he'd stumbled onto one of the lost garage bands of the sixties—except that instead of discovering this band on some scratchy record, he'd invented it himself.

When he glanced over at Lilly now, sipping coffee from a Greek diner cup, he flashed on their first night together. He'd climbed out of her bed exhausted and shaky, like he'd just ridden the Tilt-a-Whirl at the state fair. His body had been covered with creases from sleeping on her art supplies; she'd left her marks all over him.

His whole life he'd been a human Etch-A-Sketch, and he

only realized at this moment how he hated it. That's why he'd been so frustrated in all those bands, why he'd always quit after a few months. The other guys would size him up, seeming to take Hank's pale skin and white hair, his watery blue eyes, as some sign of his blankness. They'd stick him wherever they wanted—on keyboards or bass or vocal back-ups. They treated him like a studio musician.

"Hey, Hank, I thought you should play a little three-note fill here," Johnny from the Ancient Astronauts would say. "But keep it quiet. Don't compete with the guitar."

"Maybe I should improvise something bigger, you know? Make it a hook," Hank would try.

"No, no," Johnny would say. "That's not a good idea." Implying that Hank's improvisations were always stale, ripped off from old records.

Maybe that was true. But Hank had something else those guys never recognized, his own kind of genius. Who else would have taken Lilly, with her striped hats trailing from her head and her bags full of marbles and hair, and made her a lead singer? Who else would have been able to pull this bunch of misfits into a tight band, the four of them seeming to think with one mind, their songs ending with a perfect, sudden crash of silence?

Now it was Hank who held the Etch-A-Sketch and twiddled its knobs. And he knew, as if it had already happened, that he'd cut a CD someday. Maybe it would be called *Hank Alvey and the Exes,* or *The Hank Alvey Experience,* or just *Hank Alvey.* Years later, years and years later, the CD would find its way into a midwestern bedroom, to a boy hunched over his stereo who listened to the CD like he was trying to absorb this new sound through his skin, a boy who would decide right then to devote his life to the raw, crazy ache he heard, this freaky strange-ass something that bore Hank Alvey's name.

Lilly

In third grade the teacher picked her to be Mary. She stood in front of the manger, and the kids in donkey and sheep suits had to kneel around her. They were supposed to be adoring the Christ child in her arms, but Lilly knew that they kneeled around her because she was the prettiest girl in the class, with blond hair and honey skin. She kept her eyes cast upward so she'd look like the Mary at the front of the church; she'd tried to hold her fingers in that strange curled way, a girl turning into a stone.

That was the last moment of being normal she could remember. You were either normal or you had something wrong with you—foreign, ugly, fat, black, spastic, retardo, smelly. Sometime in third grade, she turned into one of the smelly ones. When her father left, the other kids could smell it on her. "You stink like a turd," they said.

Maybe she started to stink because she and her mom and her brother had to move into one of those apartment complexes where the old ladies in Woolworth dresses sat on the stairs. They stunk, those ladies. Everything stunk, and it didn't get any better until she met Ann-Marie in tenth grade. One day, Lilly heard "I Wanna Be Sedated" on Ann-Marie's Radio Shack stereo, and the most obvious, simple thought occurred to her: so what if everyone hated her? The songs on that record became her own private soundtrack; she whispered the words to herself as she walked down the halls at school.

So she and Ann-Marie invented their own punk scene in Knoxville, Tennessee; they figured out how to dress and act by studying the pictures on the back of record covers: Patti Smith, Lou Reed, Richard Hell, the Ramones, Poly Styrene, Iggy Pop, those kohl-eyed, leopard-skinned, spike-haired people from another planet. Lilly wore ripped T-shirts and black fingernail polish that she made by mixing bottles of red and blue. Ann-Marie pinned a map of New York to her wall, and with their fingers they'd roam the streets, finding where CBGB and Max's Kansas City must be hidden amid the squiggle of subway paths. Lilly always thought she'd end up there, in some tiny apartment with graffiti splattered across the walls.

But then she began writing to the lead singer of the Pricks, this amazing band up in Boston. "I saw that interview with you in *Trouser Press* and I always felt the same way about Evel Knievel. Wouldn't *Snake River* be a great name for an album?" she wrote that first time. They started out talking about motorcycles and drag racing, but after Lilly sent him a picture, they veered off into kinky jokes. "Kinky"—that was a word everyone used when Lilly was in high school, and she liked to say to people, "I've been getting these incredibly kinky letters from the lead singer of the Pricks."

When he invited her to visit, she didn't think twice. By this time, she was a freshman at the University of Tennessee. She took the bus up, and there he was waiting at the station. From the moment he took her bag and threw it in the back of his Dodge Swinger, she knew she belonged here. They went to shows every night and he introduced her to people who looked like they never left the clubs, with mushroom-colored skin and last-night's makeup still fading on their faces.

Even after she broke up with the Pricks guy, she stayed in Boston. She got a scholarship at Mass. Art. Back then a lot of the rockers were going to art school, so it didn't even occur to her that learning to draw and paint wasn't going to help her get into a band.

Anyway, she didn't necessarily have to be a rock star. It would be okay if she became famous for the cartoons she drew, or the clothes she designed, or her paintings—just as long as she became famous for *something.* Of course, it would take a while. She knew she would have to grope along toward fame, the way you fumble through a dark room, running your hands up and down the walls, until you find the light switch. And in that single instant when she finally managed to flip on the light, her life would all fall into place.

What she didn't anticipate was how long she'd have to spend groping. Every time she was about to look for a band or try and get into a gallery, the group house where she lived would break up, and then she'd have to move. And every time she did, she lost things—phone numbers, important pieces of fabric, drawings, notes, journals. Once she dreamed she was in a deserted factory building walking over brittle shards of something that crunched under her feet. All of a sudden, she realized she was trampling those precious things she'd lost over the years. They lay on the ground, glinting like broken glass, dangerous and sharp and impossible to pick up.

Sometime during all of this messed-up-ness, she burned a pink candle and concentrated on getting a guitar for free, and one day, like a miracle, she found a Gibson under a pile of junk in the basement of her group house, left there by some long-ago occupant—a guy who, a housemate said, had promised to come back and get his stuff years ago.

She took it as a sign that her luck would turn. She thought the music would flow out of her fingers as easily as the clothing designs and the drawings did. But playing the guitar was hideous. All those rules to follow, so many things to think about. She felt like Alice in Wonderland, caught in a topsy-turvy mathematical world where strange beings screamed at her. G minor, with its impossible hand position, bullied her around like the Red Queen; and E flat, one pinkie arched upward, was always angry and dull-sounding. Instead of curling into the chords, her hand clenched in painful positions. It made her cry, and she gave up.

And then she met Hank. He had the same sickness she

did, the kind that made your stomach ache whenever you heard a song you loved. Because you should have been the one who wrote it. Because it should have been yours. Hank—at least in this one way—was her twin. He too groped through the dark room, feeling for the switch that would turn everything on.

The thing was, though, he wouldn't admit how much he wanted to be famous. "Don't you want to be a rock star?" she asked him once. "Like get interviewed on MTV and have hit CDs and hang out with the Beastie Boys?"

"Are you kidding, Lill?" he said. "What's the point? You'd be forced to do crap, mainstream crap. I just want to make totally fucking impeccable music."

"Uh-huh," she said, hearing the real meaning underneath his words. He needed to be a star as badly as she did; the only difference between them was the texture and taste of the fame they craved. Lilly longed to be shot, all slit-eyed and sexy, by fashion photographers, to become Miss America in combat boots. Hank, on the other hand, longed to be secretly famous. He was obsessed with identifying the exact moment that different bands sold out to the corporate oligarchy. "I saw the Breeders in the basement of the Rat before they even had a name. They were so spontaneous and raw," he would say. "But as soon as they came out with that first CD, they turned to shit. Total la-la girl pop."

Hank wanted to belong to a band so obscure and brilliant that just knowing the name of this band would be like saying a password that got you into the secret brotherhood of the ultracool indie guys. He wanted his music to be played only on obscure college stations by snotty deejays who had piled three thousand records in their rent-controlled apartments. He wanted to get hate mail. He wanted to be a genius.

It took Lilly a while to understand all this, and to figure out what, exactly, he considered genius. At first she assumed that when Hank approved of a song, he was judging it by some musical quality she would never understand; but, no, Hank didn't care about technical skill. "That's just decoration," he'd say. Instead, he peered deep beneath the riffs and drumbeats and harmonies to discern whether or not the song had a soul.

This turned out to be the light switch Lilly had been groping for. In the glare of his vision, she suddenly understood it didn't matter how well she played; what mattered was this other nameless thing she'd had all along, her stink. It was the stink of hot dogs in a kitchen with yellow Formica counters; the stink of the Mississippi at the end of the summer when the cicadas are screaming; the stink of her own body reeking of cigarettes and incense and something sweet.

"Ever since I started practicing guitar," she told Hank, "I hear tunes in my head. Especially when I'm biking. When I'm on my bike going to work I make up entire songs with words that rhyme and everything."

"You do?" he said, excited.

"Yeah, but they're really dumb."

"Sing one for me."

She sang in just the way she did while she was biking—

high and breathy, gulping some of the words like a little kid. He began working the tune out on his keyboard and then showed her what to strum on her guitar. Soon it had turned into a real song, a miracle as amazing as the sudden appearance of the guitar itself.

"I wish I could think up stuff like that," Hank said, his voice cracking. She realized that this was a confession of his most secret shame, what he kept hidden from everyone else—his lack of soul.

"You can do it," she said. "It's easy."

"Not for me," he said.

Hank had a way of wimping out like that; he'd decide something was impossible and then he wouldn't even try. That's why she had to break up with him. "I want my boyfriend to worship me. Or if he doesn't worship me, he should at least be able to pretend he worships me," she told him once.

"I'm not going to pretend, Lilly," he said, which she thought was a very boring answer. Basically, Hank was just too self-obsessed. She needed a man who would wrap her up in fantasy like the finest mink; a man who would indulge her in all things. And then one day she was walking in the park and saw this guy lounging on a park bench with a red velvet notebook. She settled next to him and said, "I'm going to read your palm."

His love line ran in a collection of creases around the side of his hand. His mound of Mercury was pronounced and his fingers tapered elegantly, signs of a creative mind. Right from the beginning, this man—Dieter—humored her. He let her tell his fortune; he bought her a tart covered in kiwis and strawberries; he listened without interrupting. Dieter, descended in an unbroken line of blood from the Hapsburgs, spent his days brooding in his dusty apartment. He lived on a tidbit of a trust fund, occasionally taking jobs as a dog-sitter or a proofreader. That first night, she bossed him into bed with her; they made love languidly, often stopping to discuss some important point or other.

"I sometimes suddenly feel like I've slipped into another time period," Dieter said. "I'll turn a corner and from the way the leaves look, I'll know that I'm in the seventeen hundreds, say. Does that happen to you?"

"Yes," Lilly said, wiggling closer to him. "I was just realizing that we'd become people in the nineteen twenties."

"That's what I was thinking, too," he said. "We're in Berlin between the wars."

After only a few months she moved into Dieter's apartment, and it seemed like everything had ended happily ever after. She stopped losing stuff, because it all accumulated in Dieter's living room: the dressmaker's dummy, the piles of fabric, the effects boxes and patch cords. She littered his queen-sized bed with notebooks and crayons; his kitchen table became her drawing studio. Dieter didn't mind her taking over his apartment; he didn't even mind when she informed him that she was starting a band with her ex-boyfriend.

She'd come up with the concept one morning in the spring while she was drinking coffee, and had immediately called Hank. "We should name our band the Exes," she'd said breathlessly. "Because then we could have the coolest poster for our show. You know that sixties movie about wife-swapping? *Bob & Carol & Ted & Alice?* There's that picture of the four of them all in the same bed together. We could start a band that's two guys and two girls who've all slept together, and we could use that picture."

"What?" Hank had said. "What do you mean we could use the picture?"

"For our posters, I mean. When we make posters to advertise our shows. The posters would make it look like we all sleep in the same bed together." She'd had a vision of it all: the posters, the T-shirts, the band logos. Annoyingly, Hank hadn't been interested in any of the tie-in products she envisioned; instead, he kept questioning her about the Exes concept—who would have slept with whom, and what instruments would they play? But of course that's how Hank managed to get things done.

About nine months later, in the dead of winter, he booked their first gig.

"Remember that poster you thought of a while ago?" he said to her, when they took a break for a smoke one night during practice.

"What?" she said, watching how the neon of a liquor-store sign made his face look as soft and pink as a fetus's.

"You know, the *Bob & Carol & Ted & Alice* poster."

"Oh, right."

"Well, you can make it now, for our gig," he said. "We need some posters."

"Okay," she said. She took the picture of Bob & Carol &

Ted & Alice and pasted Xs over their heads. When she was finished, she had just the image she wanted: four people—each one of them with an X instead of a face—crammed into the same bed. As she walked out of the copy shop with a stack of the posters still warm from the machine, a strange sense of wonder washed over her. She'd invented the idea of this particular band with this particular poster, and it had all turned real. Though she was already twenty-nine and not famous yet, she had the sense that everything else she wanted would eventually happen, too. The thought of this scared her—spooked her, really, in the way that made the hairs on the back of her neck prickle.

During that first gig, she kept thinking, "Is this really me up here?" When she plugged in her effects boxes and tuned her guitar, she was aware of how many times she'd fantasized about exactly this moment. It weirded her out—the way she'd walked into one of her own daydreams.

The club began to fill with people holding glossy bottles of beer; most of them were here to see the headlining band, but it didn't matter. Soon they would watch her—and just this, the fact that they would be her audience, made them fascinating to her and she peered down from the stage, trying to size up each one of them.

"You guys ready?" the sound man said. The place was half full, most people clustered around the bar.

"Yeah, we're ready," Hank called over to him.

Lilly swallowed. Her spit felt like acid going down. That's how terrified she was. She glanced at the play list taped near her feet. The first song was "Splatter Movie." As if she didn't know. Hank had made them run through the set over and over.

The song started with Lilly picking her guitar, in a fast surf riff. Her stomach ached. She wasn't sure she could do it without messing up. But then Hank said, "Okay, let's go," and Walt clapped his drumsticks together, and Lilly launched into her solo. Suddenly they were in the middle of the song, and she was singing, "We'll use grapes for the eyeballs/and some ketchup for the blood./'Cause I love when your skin crawls/and your cut-off head goes thud." She was too busy singing to check out the audience, but she could sense them gathering close, their eyes like silvery beads on a black dress, their minds playing multiple movies where she was always the star.

The Exes attacked song after song with hardly a beat in between. That's how Hank wanted it. "We won't give them time to blink," he'd said. "We'll knock them on their asses." They ripped through their set in about a half an hour. To Lilly, it felt like a few seconds had gone by, a furious burst of activity and then suddenly she was shielding her eyes from the light, damp with sweat, breathless. Out there, in the dark, they were clapping and screaming.

The sound man jumped onto the stage. "What are you guys doing now? You want an encore?" Lilly realized that all of them had been just standing there, dazed.

"We don't have an encore," Hank said.

"You don't?" the guy said. "Okay, okay, let's break down." And he unplugged a cord and began winding it around his arm.

Lilly woke from her trance and lifted her guitar over her head. The audience had drifted away from the stage. She jumped down and went outside to the van. Walt and Shaz were loading the drums.

"I feel like I'm on drugs," Lilly said.

Walt glanced at her over his shoulder. "Could you hand me that stuff over there?"

Lilly lifted a pile of metal drum do-hickies and carried it over to him. Her hands felt numb. It felt like the time she smoked opium and her body turned into a giant pillow.

"I just feel really, really weird," she said.

"It's the adrenaline," Walt said. "It hangs around in your bloodstream for a while, even after you stop being scared."

Shaz backed out of the van and stood up. "I feel weird, too. Were we any good?"

"Yeah, I think so," Walt said. "Except that feedback."

"There was feedback?" Lilly asked.

"There were other fuckups, too. Like I messed up at the end," Walt said.

They kept going over what had happened, trying to piece together the reality of it from what each of them remembered. Even after they finished loading the van and had gone back inside the club, they couldn't stop analyzing their set from every angle. The next band—the headlining act—was playing, so they had to shout into each other's ears. "At least we all ended on the same beat," someone would say, or "Did they have us turned up this loud?" They all had this compulsion to know exactly what the others had been thinking on stage, as if you could add up the four streams of consciousness—the way you mixed together different instruments on a four-track—and come up with a single song of memory, a studio-produced and cleaned-up version of the truth.

This was the routine, Lilly learned after a few shows. You loaded up the van, and then you huddled together to figure out how the set had gone. After that, Lilly would drift away from the rest of the band to lean against the wall and drink free beer. People would tap her on the shoulder and yell into her ear, "That was great." It was as if they could tell how much she needed to be reassured.

That first night they performed, though, Lilly hadn't expected the postshow flurry of attention. Her friends ran up and hugged her, or kissed her on the cheek. Cool-looking strangers glanced her way. For the first time in her life, she felt like a celebrity. Late that night, some guy grabbed her elbow and ushered her over to the bar. "I need to talk to you," he said, and then he proceeded to rant about the independent film he might shoot someday and how he wanted her to play the lead.

"Would I have to memorize a lot of lines?" Lilly wanted to know.

"Oh, well, the script isn't written yet," he said, clutching his beer. "But I've got the whole thing figured out." And he proceeded to reel off the plot.

After a few months of playing out in clubs, Lilly grew used to these guys with their never-to-be-shot movies and their never-to-be-organized benefit concerts. They wanted to lay claim to you, if only in some imaginary way. For they had seen something magical glinting out of you when you were up there on stage, and they wanted credit for having such good taste. It was as if you were a rare LP on extrathick vinyl that they'd found at a yard sale for five cents—they wanted to show it to all their friends and say, "I noticed this. I noticed this when everyone else walked right by it."

On a good night, lots of people wanted you in that way. They wanted to put you in imaginary movies, plays, and bands; or they stared at you, eager to seduce you; or they tried to edge their way into the cluster of people around you. On a night like that, you felt like the coolest person in the club, but the next morning you woke up as Cinderella with a stale mouth and buzzing ears. Then you had to hustle over to the café and mop up slime from around the refrigerator and kiss-ass the customers, just like always.

So that's how it went for the first six months or so—they played around town, and it began to feel normal being on stage. The more Lilly got used to it, the more she goofed around up there. She'd stand at the mike and riff between songs: "Hey, y'all, we're the only band in the world made up entirely of people who used to go out with one another. That's right, we used to be boyfriends and girlfriends, and now instead of avoiding each other—like most of you chicken-shits out there do with your exes—we spend all our time together. At night, when we should be cuddling with our current sweetie-honeypies, we're up late jamming with our exes. And that's so we can bring you songs about love and how to get over it. Because we know how to get over it." Then she would wave the neck of her guitar in the air, and Walt would clack his drumsticks, and they'd launch into a song.

Just naturally, Lilly began hogging the spotlight, and no one seemed to mind. The rest of them were intent on play-ing—they cared more about how loud their instruments were than whether they got to talk. But Lilly knew that it didn't matter how your instruments sounded if you didn't have showmanship. That had been the secret of Elvis and Liberace and Sinatra—they way they flirted with the audi-ence. She was working on it, her showmanship, and once in a while, with a guilty twinge, she thought how she might become the true star of the act, and the Exes would turn into her backup band.

Dieter encouraged this. "They're good musicians, but you're the one who people come to watch," he told her. "They'd be just another boring band if you weren't up there working the crowd. Why don't you go solo?"

"Dieter," she had argued, "I can't go solo. Hank still has to arrange the songs for me. Besides, what's wrong with the way we are now?"

"They drown you out. I can barely hear what you're singing."

But of course that wasn't what he really meant—he just didn't like how she spent all her time with her band. He'd been totally cool at first, but after she started coming in at two in the morning all the time, he got weird. Sometimes he'd wait up for her, brooding.

"Are you mad or something?" she'd ask. "What's the problem, hon?"

"Nothing's wrong. What makes you think something's wrong?"

One weekend, the Exes got some gigs in New Hampshire and Maine; they'd decided to spend three days on a minitour. Dieter went nuts when he found out.

"I'll go with you," he said, as if he were doing her a favor.

"I really wish you could, but you can't, Dieter. There's no room in the van."

"What do you mean? Of course there's room."

"Well, not really. And where would you sleep?" she said.

"What do you mean? I'd sleep with you."

"But then we'd have to blow thirty-eight bucks each night for our own motel room. You don't want to waste that kind of money just to see more of our dumb shows, do you?"

"I don't get it," he said, crossing his arms and leaning back. "If I don't come, where do you sleep? In the van?"

"Oh, no way. We either crash on someone's floor or else we all share a motel room. That's what most bands do. Some of them do it for months while they're on tour."

He sat forward in his chair. "*Yes, but if there aren't enough beds, who are you going to be in bed with?*" he said between clenched teeth.

"I don't know." She swallowed. "Probably Hank."

"That's what I thought." He stubbed out his cigarette and glanced at her angrily.

"Dieter, calm down," she said. "I would probably sleep with him precisely because it's so totally platonic. Jesus, the very thought of fucking Hank makes my skin crawl."

"Lilly, he used to be your boyfriend. He can't make your skin crawl that much. God, how am I supposed to stand this?" Then Dieter did a weird thing. He started crying. He didn't cry the way a girl does. He just bit his lips together and tears started running out of the corners of his eyes. "This isn't going to work," he said. "We're drifting away from each other, I can tell."

"Oh don't, don't," she said. "This is just what it's like being in a band. Come here, come lie down with me."

So they lay there for a while, but just when she thought Dieter was finally okay with it, he said, "Lilly, promise me you won't."

"Oh, geez, you've got to get used to this, because we're probably going to go on a real tour someday."

"It's too weird," he said, his voice cracking.

"All right." Lilly jumped up. "I'm calling Hank right now. We're all going to talk this out." She grabbed the phone and began punching in numbers.

"No," Dieter said, trying to wrestle the receiver out of her hand. "No, stop it."

But it was too late. Within half an hour, Hank bounded up the stairs to their apartment. "Hey, man," he said. He headed for Dieter like he was going to shake his hand, but then he grabbed him around the waist and bear-hugged him. Suddenly, Lilly felt grateful for Hank's way of taking care of everything, of smoothing over hurt.

"Look, it's fine," Dieter said, his voice muffled by Hank's hug. "You didn't have to come over."

Hank steered him over to the sofa. "Don't be ashamed,

man. It's okay. I know how you feel. It sucks being in a relationship with someone in a band. But just . . . in terms of me being thrown together with Lilly a lot, you've got to believe that I have totally no interest in her at all."

"All right, I believe you. But still, why do you and Lilly have to sleep in the same bed? Why can't the guys be in one bed and the girls in another?" Dieter lit a cigarette to hide how awkward he felt.

"Look, you don't want your girlfriend in a bed with Shaz. Take my word for it. She's a friggin' dyke, man." Hank put his arm around Dieter's shoulder, a just-between-guys gesture that turned what he said into a joke.

"Yeah." Dieter smiled in spite of himself. "Yeah, I forgot. You think Shaz would try to convert her?"

"Are you kidding? Don't you know what the dykes are up to? They've got these underground tunnels, man. They meet down there and plot how to get at all the straight girls. The dykes are our true enemies, not each other. You and me, we've got to stick together."

Dieter was actually in a good mood now. "You're right. If our girlfriends find out what it's like to sleep with women, it's all over for us."

"You got it, man. It's like when a shark tastes blood. Once a chick tastes pussy juice, she'll turn on you. You want that to happen? Your want Lilly to come home with *The SCUM Manifesto* in one hand and a knife in the other?"

Lilly laughed. It was brilliant, Hank bonding with Dieter this way. Usually Hank talked to other guys about indie bands or rare vinyl, but with Dieter that wasn't an option, so he'd picked the one thing he knew they had in common. Hank was going on and on about pussy, but he was doing it in this parody of crudeness. It was as if Hank were saying to Dieter, "Hey, we're both sensitive guys here. But underneath, underneath all this political correctness, we're still he-men. And if we ever really wanted to, we could stop acting wimpy and start ordering our women around."

So Dieter calmed down, everything was cool, and that Friday the Exes loaded the van and drove north. It wasn't a real tour, just a few gigs at tiny clubs—a trial run, a way to figure out if they wanted to save up their money and go on tour for a few months. At least that's how she and Hank thought of it.

"Keep it mellow when you talk to Shaz, okay?" Hank told Lilly when he called her up to give her last-minute instructions before the trip. "Act like we're just doing this for fun. Don't let on that we're planning our Victory tour."

"Well, duh," Lilly said into the phone. "Don't you think she's figured out by now that we want to be famous?"

"I'm just thinking if we ease her in . . ."

"Whatever," Lilly said. There was no point in telling him. He would just get paranoid if he knew that she'd been hanging out with Shaz for a while now. They met at the Other Side café, and they bitched about the whole guy-rock thing. Lilly figured that these bitch sessions were what kept Shaz in the band.

The last time, Shaz had stared down at her frothy wheat-grass juice and run a finger over the beads of sweat on the glass. Then she'd stared up at Lilly. "You have no idea how much it can suck when it stops being just for fun. When there's contracts and tours and sleazebags promising you money."

"Doesn't sound so bad to me," Lilly had said, taking another swig from her beer.

"People change once they think they're going to get famous. Some people—they'll turn on you." Shaz darted her eyes toward Lilly then away, like she wanted to tell a secret but didn't dare. Lilly found herself leaning forward, hands out as if to grab the words from Shaz's mouth. "I've gotten burned," Shaz said.

"What happened exactly? You never tell me the details."

Shaz fixed her with those black-hole eyes. "I'm not trying to hide anything. It's just . . . I'm not good at explaining. When I was in Sluggo, all the rest of those guys, they would do anything to get a CD contract or whatever. They didn't care about what I wanted. I felt used, really."

"But what happened?"

Shaz shrugged. "It was a lot of things, you know?"

"Goddamn," Lilly blurted out. "You're such a tease. No wonder everyone's got a crush on you."

"What are you talking about?" Shaz laughed uncomfortably.

"Like right now," Lilly said. "You're being so damn fascinating. You're telling me some big drama went on in Sluggo, but you won't tell me what it was. You've got me totally hooked in."

Shaz fixed her eyes on Lilly's. "I'm just trying to say it can turn out badly. I like you, Lilly, and I don't want you to get mad at me if I quit this band."

Lilly raised her hand in the air, fist cocked, two fingers poking upward. "Scout's honor. I won't get mad." And then, because she knew Shaz loved secrets, loved complicity and private pacts, she added, "We won't tell anyone else, but we'll keep meeting every few weeks, okay? We'll stick together and we won't ever let Hank drive us apart, no matter what."

Shaz met her eyes. "You promise?"

"Yeah," Lilly said, relieved to have finally figured out how to control Shaz. You couldn't tie her to you with heavy ropes; you had to use hundreds of spiderwebs instead. You had to sew her to you with invisible thread and a needle made out of glass.

You had to remember that Shaz had been there, done that. She'd experienced some minor rock-star fame, and even gone on a two-week tour with Sluggo, which she'd hated. "It's not like you're imagining, Lilly," she said. "I spent most of the time riding in a truck with no windows, trying not to throw up." Lilly had nodded, but hadn't believed her. Of course touring was glamorous, every minute of it.

Later, she found out that there was something to what Shaz was saying. Even on that first weekend tour, Lilly began to see how it could suck. They drove for hours and then they had to sit around forever waiting to play. Since it was February, they couldn't go outside much. In Dover, New Hampshire, they had to hang out in a Store 24 for about an hour while Hank tried to reach the guy who'd booked them.

But once they started to play, everything turned out great. At this one coffeehouse in Portland, they tried the walkie-talkie song for the first time; Lilly grabbed the Fisher-Price toy and ran into the men's bathroom with it. She kept singing from in there, the door slightly open so she could watch how the Exes moved around the empty spot where she usually stood and how the other walkie-talkie dangled against the mike—then, just at the right moment, she ran out and climbed up on a table, screaming the lyrics into that stupid-looking pink walkie-talkie with such passion that she knew she transcended the gimmicky-ness and dopeyness of the whole situation. And when they ended the song with a crash of drums, the audience was screaming so loud you thought they might burst some blood vessels. The Exes did five encores that night. Later, a deejay from one of the radio stations took their tape and promised to show it around, and people mobbed Walt to buy their T-shirts. Out here in the hinterland, nobody knew how low they ranked in the Boston scene; nobody knew the Exes were just another Sunday-night-at-the-Midway, totally obscure band. Out here they were gods.

After the show, Hank went out for drinks with some local rock dudes, and the rest of them drove to the Motel 6. It was the first night they'd stayed in a motel; in the other towns, they'd managed to crash on people's floors. Lilly loved it, coming back to a motel. The night before, they'd slept on the floor of a freezing cold house. Except they never really got to sleep because their host and all his roommates wanted to sit around drinking Meister Brau and shooting the shit all night—which to them meant ranting on and on about their stupid local scene and the stupid band they might start. After that, one shared motel room seemed luxurious.

Lilly even got her own bed—at least it was hers until Hank slipped under the covers in the middle of the night.

"Hi," she whispered, so as not to wake Shaz and Walt.

"Hey," he whispered back. "That was a great show."

"Yeah," she said, opening her eyes a crack to take in the dark lump of him on the other side of the bed. "This is a little weird."

"What's weird?" Hank said.

"Us sharing a bed. It's like we've suddenly gone back in time."

"Naw. Just don't think about that."

"Okay," she said and started to drift off.

After a few minutes, he suddenly whispered, "But it is funny. You know, I was just thinking. When we used to sleep together, your bed was always full of all that junk, scissors and glue and paper clips and stuff. Remember?"

"Yeah. My bed's still like that."

"There was so much stuff in there, I'd always wake up with something lodged in my side or poking into my butt. And now here we are in this totally clean motel bed."

"It's good, isn't it? Everything's clean between us. Clean slate," Lilly said, breathing in the scent of starch and moving her legs a little to appreciate the yards and yards of fresh cotton. No grit, no plastic toys, no wads of paper, no smell of sweat.

"Yeah, everything's so simple now," Hank said, sounding drunk and half asleep.

Near morning, Lilly woke to find him wrapped around her. He'd snaked one hand under her T-shirt and he had his head wedged into the crook of her neck. She lay there for a minute noticing the differences between him and Dieter. Hank was more muscular, more all-American. His arm fit neatly in the dip of her waist and his chest clamped to her back. He held her purposefully in those slim, sinewy arms of his. Dieter usually just curled against her like a cat. He wasn't the best sleeping partner. He woke in the middle of the night and wandered around the apartment; he yanked the blankets away from her, as if she were part of some conspiracy to keep him cold. And he rarely held her like Hank did. She'd forgotten how much she missed it.

Even though she knew she should roll away from Hank, she didn't. She fell asleep like that, thinking, "Dieter wouldn't understand. It's not sex, it's comfort." When she woke up the next morning, Hank was on the other side of the bed, sprawled across his pillow, Shaz and Walt were in the bathroom, arguing in whispers, and everything was back to normal.

"I don't want to go back," Hank yelled over the roar of the van later that day. "I wish we could just keep driving around."

"I don't want to go back either," Walt said. "It's like we lived out our fantasy."

"Yeah," Shaz said. "I wasn't so hot on the idea of going away all weekend, but it turned out to be okay."

"I just can't friggin' stand it that we're going to be right back in Boston, playing on Sunday nights to twenty people again," Hank said. "We're way too good for that."

For a while Lilly bobbed next to him in the backseat of the van, depressed. Hank was right—in Boston, they were totally considered an amateur-hour band. And then suddenly she had a vision, a hilariously weird vision. She doubled up in a painful fit of giggles, grabbing Walt's seat so she wouldn't fall over.

Walt, in the driver's seat, glanced back at her. "What? What?"

"I know what to do," Lilly said, gasping for air. Her eyes were tearing. She felt on the verge of hysteria. "We'll be like a league of superheroes, okay? Like one of those superhero rock bands on Saturday-morning TV. You know, like the four kids in *Scooby Doo.*"

"They weren't a rock band," Walt said.

"Okay, then we'll be like the rock band in *Lancelot Link, Secret Chimp.*"

"What do you mean? You want us to act like talking chimps?" Walt asked.

"No, no. In *Lancelot Link,* Lancelot and all his friends were in a rock band, right? But they were also spies. We'll be like that. We'll be musicians, but we'll also have our secret identities. Because what we've been forgetting is that it's not enough to just play music. We have to have a whole myth, like, a mission." Lilly was growing serious now, getting caught up in her own logic. "We each need to be a su-perhero."

Walt looked over at her. "What's my superhero iden-tity?"

"You're Tech Man," she said, without missing a beat. "Your secret power is transporting us in the van and setting up equipment, and knowing about electronics and stuff. Shaz, you're . . . um, you're Common-Sense Girl. You're the only one among us with a lick of sense. Hank is Gig Boy. He knows everyone on the scene; he gets us gigs and makes deals and stuff. I'm Promo Girl. I'm going to send out tapes to everyone at the radio stations and think up PR stunts."

"Well, like, if we're superheroes, do we have to fight crime or something?" Walt said. "I mean, would there be an evil rock band bent on world domination that we would have to go head-to-head with?"

"No, we're not the kind of superheroes who save people," she said. "We're just superheroes who make ourselves fa-mous."

Everybody else forgot about their superhero identities. But not Lilly—she spent hours and hours being Promo Girl. She'd send out thick packages full of demo tapes and toys. Or she would call deejays; she'd look them up in Infor-mation and catch them at home. Once she transformed her-self into Promo Girl, she'd do anything for the band. She'd call anyone and say anything. It was her prime directive.

Dieter hated it when she turned into Promo Girl. He would sulk at the other end of the apartment, pretending to read philosophy. When she finally came over to talk to him, he'd shrink back. "Calm down," he'd say. "You're acting like you're trying to sell me something. Just, could you please talk in a normal voice?"

The truth was, things hadn't been the same with Dieter since that weekend she'd gone up north. He started acting like the band was no big deal, just some little hobby of hers. She didn't want him to slobber over her like a fan, she just wished he could be happy for her. "Hey, so guess what?" she might tell him. "I called this guy from the *Phoenix* and he might do an interview with me. He says he's seen the band and he really likes us."

"Oh, great, Lill," Dieter would say, glancing up from his book. "It's too bad the *Phoenix* is such a rag, though. You deserve better."

And then, as if that wasn't bad enough, this horrible new development occurred: Dieter and Hank became best friends. Lilly didn't even know they'd been hanging out, and then one night she walked in the door and there they were, sprawled on the sofa together. She felt panicky, like she wanted to turn around and run out the door.

"Hey, bitch," Dieter called, his voice strangely high. "You sho' look fine."

She took a few steps into the living room. "What?" she said. "What did you call me?"

The two of them were sharing a forty-ounce bottle of malt liquor and watching some movie on the VCR.

"Yo' my bitch," Dieter said, in that strange, forced voice. He was acting so out of character that she felt dizzy.

"Hey, mama," Hank called, "come here and get loaded with us."

"What's y'all's problem?" Lilly glanced at the movie they were watching—black people with huge Afros, wearing polyester.

"It's *Superfly*," Hank said, "I've been wanting to see this for a long time. So I came over and kind of forced it on Dee."

All of a sudden, Lilly understood what had happened. In their minds they'd turned into two black pimps of the seventies, lounging around and getting buzzed on malt liquor, entering into a mellow horniness together. Of course, it was all Hank's doing. Hank had invented a new personality for Dieter. He kept calling him Dee. "Hey, don't Bogart that cigarette, Dee," he'd say. Or, "Dee, Dee, check out that chick."

Dieter—the Dieter she knew—only watched movies with subtitles, Fassbinder or Cocteau. But Dee, this stranger on the sofa, leaned forward to catch every frame of *Superfly*, his head lolling because he was sloppy drunk.

"He's slapping her around," Dee said, his eyes on the screen.

"Yeah, great, that's a real hoot," Lilly said. But then, not knowing what else to do, she sat down between the two of them. Dieter started fondling her thigh. "Lilly's got some meat on her," he said to Hank. "Look at how strong her legs are."

"Yeah, I liked that too," Hank said, laughing kind of hysterically. "Tall girls with long legs. That's what I'm into."

And so there she sat, with Dieter holding on to her leg and Hank leaning against her shoulder. She had to admit that she got off on it—these two guys touching her and talking about her body. But she was on edge, too. She half expected some horrible scene by the end of the night. All that happened, though, was Hank passed out on the sofa, and she threw a blanket over his curled-up body before she went to sleep.

Things only got worse. Dieter and Hank drove up to Lynn to see Trucks in the Mud that weekend; the next week they went to the new Schwarzenegger movie together, and Dieter came home in this bizarre hyper state, where he kept turning his fingers into a machine gun and blowing everything away.

The worst was one day when Dieter suddenly started wearing this jacket that seemed oddly familiar. "Wait a sec, where'd you get that?" Lilly fingered the gas station–attendant windbreaker. It had an oval name tag on it that said DICK.

"Hank didn't want it anymore so he gave it to me."

"Oh, geez," Lilly said. "I *broke up* with Hank and now you're turning into him."

"I am not. You just can't deal with it if I have my own friends. You want everything to revolve around you, Lilly, but that's not fair. I have to have my own life."

"Fine," Lilly yelled. "Then get your own. Why did you have to pick Hank? Now everything *is* revolving around me in a way I totally hate."

They'd both sulked at opposite ends of the apartment after this fight. Lilly sat there working on a collage and trying to figure out what had happened. She used to be the powerful one in this relationship, and now everything had flipped. She needed a plan to get back in control again, but she couldn't think of one.

Things turned really twisted a few nights later, when they were having dinner at Hank's house. The guys had gotten buzzed, and they'd started talking about Deb—who Hank was in the process of breaking up with.

"She was never that good a girlfriend anyway. She didn't give me blow jobs all the time, like Lilly did."

"Shut up, Hank, I did not."

"You gave him blow jobs all the time?" Dieter said. "What happened? Why am I getting ripped off?"

"No, you're just getting bullshitted," she'd said, trying to keep her voice normal, trying to pretend the air wasn't crackling with dangerous sparks. The best thing, maybe, was to ignore it. "Tell me what's going on at the store," she said to Hank. "Did they give you more money?"

And it worked. Hank turned back into the guy she knew. He sighed. "No, they're not going to promote me. And Sean's still away, so I'm doing his job, too. Hey, Dee, what is this? You're taking all the spaghetti. Give me some."

"Me too," Lilly said, holding out her plate.

"Hey, man, what's going on with the noodle-to-sauce ratio? You're giving me a very low ratio there," Hank said.

That's how it was when it was good, like they were family. It lasted that way all through dinner, and in the dim glow of Hank's kitchen, with its steamy air and smell of oregano, she began to relax again.

When she stood up to clear the plates and tried to wedge past Hank, he grabbed her, pulling her down into his lap.

"Hey, Lilly girl," he said. He rocked her back and forth on his knees. "How's my sweetie?"

She laughed. "You're going to make me fall off!"

"I won't let you fall off. Just relax," Hank said, and then his voice changed. "I'm in a prime position to grab her tits, man," he called to Dieter.

"No way," Dieter said, stumbling over. He was laughing, they were all laughing. Lilly was laughing in spasms, like she had dry heaves.

"You're not allowed," Dieter said. "She's mine."

"I'll pay you. How much would I have to pay to feel her tits?"

"Um, how about a dollar."

"A dollar for each tit or for both?"

"You can have both for a dollar."

"Okay, it's a deal," Hank said, grabbing at Lilly's chest.

"Hank," she screamed, and struggled free. "You two are being so obnoxious." She stalked out into the living room and then, her heart still hammering, pretended to look through Hank's records.

"Lilly," they called to her. "Lilly, don't be mad. We didn't mean it."

Even when she and Dieter got home, she didn't feel like she was alone with him. The ghost of Hank hovered in the corner, over by the pile of dirty clothes—somewhere like that, just at the edge of her vision.

Dieter propped himself next to her in bed and kneaded her back. "It's weird that he's breaking up with Deb, even though they're not fighting."

Lilly grunted. "Yeah, I guess." She was concentrating on his fingers circling under her shoulder blades. She could tell Dieter was trying to get her out of her bad mood.

"That's not what happened with you and Hank, is it?" Dieter said. "You guys fought a lot, huh?"

"Yeah."

"So"—his voice got high here—"what was it like having sex with him? I mean, did you really give him blow jobs all the time?"

"Oh, please," she said, and rolled over. "Would you stop?"

She didn't think too much about any of this until a few days later. She was at the café, trying to clean dried milk off the steamer; the milk became all Styrofoamish when it was dry and she was scraping it with a knife, when all of a sudden she felt really pissed off, like she wanted to plunge the knife into the next person who walked by. She had to stand up and stare into space for a minute—sorting around in her mind the way you'd sort through junk in a box—before she found the reason. It was Dieter selling her tits to Hank for a dollar. She couldn't believe that had happened.

She went outside for a smoke break. What she didn't understand was why she always went along with their stupid game. Why had she let Hank pull her down into his lap? Because she hadn't expected the bad scene that would follow—just the opposite, she had thought something wonderful was about to happen. Circled by Hank's arms, with Dieter scraping the plates and giving off a comfortable domestic vibe, she had a momentary vision of what it would be like to be loved by both of them—not just that, to be loved by all men. She'd felt like she sometimes did on stage, bathing in love like it was an endless supply of warm water.

When she and Dieter first started going out, he'd made her feel like that. He had cared for her, obsessed about her. "Here, Lilly, you eat my eggs because you never get enough protein," he would say. He'd been all worried about her health; he couldn't stand that she lived on coffee, cake, and cigarettes. "I bought you a present," he said once when she walked in the door. "A special pillow so you won't get neck aches." It was as if he trained a spotlight on her, scrutinizing her every comment, her slightest gesture—she'd never felt so understood by another person in her life before.

But it hadn't been like that for a long time. Nowadays when she came over and tried to kiss him, to push herself into his lap, he's say, "Hey, I'm reading." The more she tried to get his attention, the more she ended up annoying him.

Lilly stubbed out her cigarette and went back inside. As she made lattes and sponged off counters, she meditated on her relationship, trying to figure it out. It hovered in her mind like a complex pattern for a dress she was altering. How would she handle the darts and hems? How would she put it all together again so the seams wouldn't show? By the time she biked home, she had it all worked out. She knew exactly what to say to him.

Later that night, while Dieter lay soaking in the tub, she sat on the toilet and tried to explain. "Look," she said, "I'm not blaming you, but I think that you and Hank treat me in this really bad way sometimes. It's like, in order for you guys to be such close friends, you have to make fun of the whole situation—I mean, that you've both slept with me. But the thing is, instead of the situation, you end up making fun of *me.*"

"What?" He took a drag from his cigarette and then put it back on the edge of the tub. "Explain that again," he said, ultracalm, not quite looking at her.

She tried. She went at it from every angle.

"You're going to get mad at me, Lil," he said. "But this is my interpretation: You feel upset whenever you're not the center of attention. You don't like it that Hank and I have our own friendship."

"No, you *do* make fun of me," she whined, sounding desperate now. She tried to list the bad things he had said, how he had hurt her, but she couldn't seem to remember it right.

"Come here," Dieter said, raising one soapy arm out of the water. She sat on the edge of the tub. "Honeypie, you're so sensitive," he said, stroking her knee with his wet hand. "I'll try to be more careful, okay?"

"Okay," she said and rolled her eyes.

That was the moment she decided to give up on Dieter and work on Hank. If only she could get Hank on her side, everything would be different. She didn't understand how it had happened, but the dynamic of her relationship with

Dieter was this: whoever Hank liked better was the powerful one.

It reminded her of when she was a kid, how she fought with her brother over who really owned their dog, Baby. She and her brother used to put Baby in the middle of the yard and then they'd each stand at opposite ends and call her. Lilly remembered yelling, "Baby, Baby, come here, come *here*," so urgently that she thought she'd pop a vein in her forehead. What did it prove, making Baby come to you instead of your brother? It proved that you were the *real* master of Baby, because neither she nor her brother believed that a dog could belong to two kids at the same time. Lassie didn't have two masters. Old Yeller didn't have two masters. Baby had to pick a master, and if she picked Lilly, it would prove once and for all that Lilly was more lovable. That's not how it turned out, though. In the end, Baby began prancing around after her brother Todd. That hurt. Especially because Todd would say stuff like "Don't push Baby into your room. She wants to sleep in here with me. She sleeps here every night." Now, it was like Hank was her and Dieter's dog—and this time she was determined to be the one who was more lovable.

She had this whole plan. She'd nab Hank after practice, take him to a bar and get him drunk. Then she'd explain how she felt. Hank was reasonable; he'd understand.

But the next day, what with all the excitement, Lilly forgot about her plan. When she got home, a guy from the Fabric Factory had left a message on her machine. "Listen," he said, in a gravelly, nonchalant voice, "one of the bands we had booked just dropped out on us. I really liked that tape and all those promo materials you sent, so I was wondering if you guys could fill in on the twenty-seventh. You'd open for the Satanistas."

Lilly started screaming like she'd just picked the right door on *Let's Make a Deal*. She squealed and ran around in a circle and bit her fist, and then she called all the other Exes, and she left a message at the Fabric Factory, and then she hustled to work.

All the rest of the day she ran around mopping and wiping and steaming milk in an adrenaline high, the fame fantasies quick-cutting in her head like MTV videos. The Fabric Factory was big time—bands like Come and the Breeders and Redd Kross. The Satanistas were big time, too—they'd invented this new form of music, a sort of cocktail-lounge version of heavy metal. Record-label guys would probably be at this gig, and reviewers, too.

For the next two weeks, Lilly barely saw Dieter, except when she slid into bed next to his body. She didn't have time to concentrate on her relationship problems, what with practice to go to and a work schedule to rearrange and all the rest of it. And then, on the day of the gig, as they were all climbing into the van, it struck her that this—this long ride into New York—would be the perfect opportunity to talk to Hank. "Hey, sit in the back with me," she said, and grabbed his arm so he'd slide onto the bench seat beside her.

He was still all hyper. "We didn't forget the walkie-talkies, did we?" he said as they pulled out onto 93. Then he leaned over the seat and began riffling through the odds and ends in a milk crate.

"Calm down. We've got everything. You need to chill out," Lilly said. They were passing the gas tank on the outskirts of Boston, the one that looked like a giant roll of toilet paper. Years ago, someone had painted swatches of color across the tank. "Do you see the picture of Ho Chi Minh?" she said.

"What?" Hank squinted in the direction where she pointed.

"It's this legend: Supposedly whoever painted that gas tank hid the giant face of Ho Chi Minh in the blue stripe. It was an antiwar protest, though not a very effective one if you ask me."

"I'll say." Hank already seemed to be relaxing. "If it's supposed to be Ho Chi Minh, I don't think it's very flattering. Looks more like just some splattery blob. Some Rorschach test."

"Yeah, I know. Hey, do you want a Little Debbie Jelly Triangle?" she said. "I call them Bermuda Triangles because the jelly spurts out and gets all over you. It's like a toxic spill. Be careful."

So she buttered him up like that, and by the time they were zipping by the ultraclean insurance-esque buildings of Hartford, she got up the courage to say, "Hank, do you think there's something weird going on between you and me and Dieter?"

"Huh?" he said, lifting his head off his arm. "What do you mean?"

"Remember that night when me and Dieter came over to your house?"

He didn't remember, and she had to fill him in. "Oh God, that's right," he said. "I can't believe I grabbed you like that." He slapped himself in the forehead. "Uggh, stupid me. I was so wasted."

"It just—that made me feel terrible. Like you'd turned against me."

"Yeah, I guess it was crass. I'm sorry, Lilly. I really just meant it as a joke."

"I know. It's not your fault. It's me and Dieter. Things aren't great between us now. So when he starts talking about selling my tits, I can't exactly take it as a joke. I mean, in the back of his mind, he really does think he owns me."

"Oh geez, I'm sorry it's like that. Have you talked to him?"

"Yeah. It doesn't do any good. But anyway, I wanted to ask you a favor. When we're all together, don't let that weird stuff happen, okay? You guys kind of put on this manly act, where you start being all crude or whatever. I know *you're* just kidding, Hank, but there's some part of it that Dieter takes seriously."

Hank ran a hand through his hair. "Now I feel really terrible. Lilly, I'm sorry. It's true that Dieter and me get raunchy when we're together. I guess we've both been having relationship troubles, and it's a messed-up way of dealing. Things have been hard for me, too, Lilly. Awful. But that's no excuse for acting like a pig."

"What's going on?"

"Deb and I keep trying to break up, but then there she is, living in the apartment above me, so we end up sleeping together again. It's confusing as hell. Then Dieter appears out of nowhere and wants to be my best friend. That's what's saved my life. So, I don't know, I guess Dee and I sometimes get into this women-suck, we-guys-are-all-in-it-together head space, you know."

"Yeah, that's okay. You can hate women sometimes if you want. Just don't hate me, okay?"

"Okay, Lilly. I know what. Let's shake on it. The X handshake."

"What? Oh yeah." She started laughing. "I forgot about that."

They started shaking and then held the Vs of their fingers interlocked for a few seconds longer than they had to. At the center of the X shake, where the crotch of her fingers touched the skin between Hank's fingers, she felt an electricity. The place in between your fingers: you never think about it, but it's one of the most tender bits of flesh, as private as the inside of your thighs or the folds of your ear. She liked feeling joined to Hank there.

"You're one of the few people I trust," she said. She meant, though she didn't know how to explain it right, that Hank was predictable in his way. Which was a relief after Dieter, with his angst and tantrums.

Later—when they were sitting in the Fabric Factory bar, waiting for a sound check—Lilly lay her head on her arms and thought about Dieter. She wished there was one moment she could identify, one incident she could point to and say, "That's where all the bad feeling started." But it wasn't like that really, like something good had turned bad. Maybe she'd never known Dieter. In the beginning she'd thought she did, thought she saw him the way she used to think she could pick out Ho Chi Minh on that gas tank. But nowadays when she drove past the tank, she realized that the slash of blue paint wasn't Ho's goatee after all; there was no face, just a random splatter of paint. It was the same with Dieter. She couldn't see his face; he was all splatter and no pattern.

"Lilly." Walt was standing behind her. "You have the keys to the van, right?"

She got up. "Yeah. Here. Oh geez, I'm not into this show. What if I totally suck and we've come all the way down here for nothing?" Suddenly she was in a panic.

"I'll help you." Walt sat down opposite her. "I'm learning how to hypnotize people. I've been reading about it—it's this really interesting physiological state."

"No, come on, leave me alone," she said.

"Stare into my eyes." He leaned toward her and opened his own eyes as wide as they would go.

"You look like a lunatic," she said.

"Come on, stare into my eyes," he said, and there was something about his stupid enthusiasm that was irresistible. She stared back at him. Opening her eyes as wide as she could made her feel like a little kid.

"You're relaxed and confident," he said, in a monotone. "You can't wait to get on stage."

She tried to hold his stare, but she started cracking up. "Oh God, Walt, this is dopey."

"See, it worked," he said. "You're in a better mood already."

She felt a wave of affection for him, good old Walt who drove the van everywhere without a complaint, who wanted to make her happy even if he didn't know how.

And maybe Walt's hypnotism did work. Because later, when she stood in the glare of lights, testing out her effects boxes and trying not to glance out at the audience, she knew this would be an amazing show. The rest of the band slipped into readiness around her. Now she had the magic power. She could see in 360 degrees—without turning around, she knew that Walt had balanced his sticks delicately on top of his high hat, and that Shaz had hunched over her bass, and that Hank—off to her side—had his foot poised over the flanger box.

Then Walt's drumsticks cracked, and suddenly they were in the middle of a song. "Baby, baby, don't tilt the machine. It's the best one I've ever seen," Lilly was singing. "Hit flippers, keep the ball in play. One wrong move will give it all away." They'd added a new bit—after the second chorus, they suddenly morphed the song into "Pinball Wizard" for a few bars and then morphed back into their own song.

"Tilt, tilt, tilt, tilt, tilt," Lilly screamed. And they came crashing into silence.

She heard clapping and screaming, but she couldn't see them out there. "Hey, thank you," Lilly said into the mike, and the noise died down. "We're the Exes, and we all used to be girlfriends and boyfriends with each other." She went into her Exes spiel. By now it had become as automatic as the songs themselves.

Over the months, she'd added a lot of patter, including a whole new band-introduction thing. "Okay," Lilly said, while the band backed her up with an instrumental, "first I want to tell you who I am. My name is Miss Lilly Major and I'm a Scorpio." She launched into a guitar solo, rocked out for a minute, and then added, "My favorite color is mauve, and my turn-ons are Beatle boots, sideburns, and honesty. On the bass is Shaz Dohra."

Right on cue, Shaz started into her solo; after a minute, Lilly continued: "Shaz is the Aries lady of our group. Her favorite drink is a Suffering Bastard, and she's turned on by gray hair, leather pants, and a woman's right to choose." Shaz stopped popping her bass and settled down into a thrumming beat so Lilly could talk again.

"On the drums"—Lilly pointed behind her—"is our man Walter Blume. Waltie is a Virgo, a scientific genius, and perhaps the only member of the Exes who is truly employable. He's so mysterious that I have no idea what his turn-ons are. You're going to have to find out for yourselves, ladies."

After Walt's solo, she took the mike again. She could tell that she *had* the audience. She was leading them around on a leash like a little pooch. "Over here on lead guitar and keys is Mr. Hank Alvey, my own personal ex. Hank is a Taurus and he's stubborn as all get-out. He likes ladies with long legs and big ol' record collections."

Hank hammered on his guitar for a minute, and then they all joined in, finding each other and chugging into the final song.

Then they ran off the stage, huddling by the bar while the audience screamed for an encore. "Where's the walkie-talkie?" Lilly yelled into Hank's ear. He ran up on stage and—taking himself superseriously—duct-taped the pink Fisher-Price toy to the mike. Lilly knew just what to do; she ran to her bag of stuff and found her paper Burger King crown. Then, just at the right moment, she bounded onto the stage and shoved the paper crown on her head.

She was singing into her bubble-shaped walkie-talkie, dancing around the stage, letting the crowd get used to the staticky, man-on-the-moon sound of her voice. Then she leapt down from the stage brandishing her walkie-talkie and ran through clusters of people. She sang from the back of the club, then squeezed through the door and burst out into the cool of a New York street, traffic whizzing by and honking and rumbling all around. She paced down the street, holding the walkie-talkie to her ear until she couldn't hear the Exes anymore, only the hiss of space. Then she leaned against a building and had a smoke.

Afterward, when she ducked back into the club, some guy stopped her. "Hey, that was amazing," he said, leaning one arm against the wall, looking down at her.

"Thanks," she said, about to slip by him.

"I'm Andrew from the Satanistas. I hope you guys can stay and see our set."

"Oh yeah, oh wow." Lilly ran one hand through her dreads. "We're big fans."

"I'd actually never heard of you guys. Do you have anything out? Are you signed with anyone?"

"No, no. We're pretty obscure."

"Well, maybe . . . I mean, why don't you give me a tape and I'll play it for some people. See what I can do."

"Let me find my bag," she said, and she led him backstage.

"Hey," he said, as she fished around trying to find the tape. "Did you notice I have sideburns?"

"Huh? Sideburns?" she said, handing it to him.

"Your turn-on. Sideburns."

"Oh yeah," she smiled. "They're beautiful." She reached over and touched the curly, stiff hair next to one ear. And then he was called off to his sound check.

After the show, Shaz and Walt said they'd park the van in Brooklyn in some private driveway their friend had. They dropped Lilly and Hank off at Hank's brother's apartment. The brother answered his door half asleep, opened up the living-room futon for them, and then said, "I'm going back to bed, you guys. I have to be up at six."

Hank paced around. "What can we do, Lilly? I'm all keyed up, but we can't go out or we'd wake up Rod again."

"Let's drink."

Hank hunted until he found a bottle of whiskey. They

passed it back and forth as they wandered around the room snooping through Rod's stuff.

She took a swig and it burned in her throat like sugar. "What do you figure Shaz and Walt are doing right now?"

"Picking their noses."

"Maybe they're getting it on." Lilly started laughing so hard she was snorting.

"Don't be so juvenile," Hank said, peering into Rod's closet.

"I'm feeling juvenile. Listen, do you think Walt's still in love with her? I do."

Hank shook his head. "She's got a new girlfriend anyway."

"You'd do her, wouldn't you?"

"Shaz?" he said, voice cracking a little. "I've never really gotten along with her that well, but sure. I'd do her."

"How come everyone's in love with her? She's kind of flabby. Her legs are skinny but her stomach sticks out." Lilly laughed. She felt like she could say anything tonight.

"I think she's pretty cute."

"It's her eyes. She got those bedroom eyes. It's like she shoots X-ray beams of lust at you," Lilly said meditatively. "I want to be like that."

"You're sexy in a different way." Now Hank leaned against the wall, facing her. "She's Veronica and you're Betty."

"I don't want to be Betty." Lilly flopped down on the futon.

"What's wrong with you, Lill? Why are you so insecure?" he said, his voice sounding suddenly tender. "You were great tonight—it was amazing when you ran out of the club. Aren't you psyched the show went so well?"

"I'm scared," she said. "Something's going to happen for us soon. I know what's next, Hank. We're going to hit it big."

"Yeah," he said, flopping down beside her. "I can feel it, too."

Lilly pulled a pillow under her head. "That guy from the Satanistas, Andrew, he might help us. He wanted our tape. And I could tell he had a total crush on me."

"He had a crush on you?" Hank's voice was sharp. He rolled over to look at her. "Suddenly, for some stupid reason, I'm jealous," he said.

"Really? Cool."

"Yeah. I'm never jealous of Dieter. But I'm jealous of that Satanista guy, because he can see. . . . He understands how amazing you are on stage. I'm scared he'll want you to be in his band. Lilly, one of these days somebody's going to try to steal you away. I don't want you to leave me."

She turned serious. "I won't, Hank. I swear I won't. I've been thinking lately about this whole rock-star thing. It's dumb really." She glanced over at him, flat on his back beside her on the bed. This was like one of those talks she used to have with her best friend Ann-Marie when they slept over at each other's houses in high school.

"Dumb? You've worked your butt off for it."

"I know, but all this hell with Dieter, it's worn me out. I just, like, want to have my boyfriend and my band, and not have my whole life falling apart. I mean, what if Dieter and me break up?" She heard her voice crack. "What will I do?"

"I'll make sure you're okay," Hank said. He was lying beside her, and she didn't so much hear his words as feel them through the futon, like magic fingers.

"Are you sure?" she said, still gazing up at the ceiling.

Hank leaned over, staring intently into her eyes. "I used to think you were so wild. But you're the one person who's always been there for me."

"No duh," she said, laughing, pushing on his chest like she was trying to knock him off the bed.

And then his arms just kind of gave out underneath him. He fell on top of her and kissed her, sending a whiff of whiskey into her mouth like a flame.

"You've got the devil's tongue." She giggled.

And neither of them said, "We shouldn't be doing this," but those words floated around them like ghosts, thin and vapory and easy to ignore.

He sucked her boob through her shirt, and she remembered how he used to do that; and there was comfort in the long-ago familiar gestures of his lust. Soon they lay naked under the spotlight of a halogen light—Lilly thought of reaching up to turn it off, but didn't. That would be like admitting that she was doing something wrong.

Hank reached over to his wallet and pulled out a condom. He grinned crookedly. "This thing has been in here for months."

"Sure, sure." She laughed.

And then they were fucking in a frenzy, their bodies slick against each other. She and Dieter had a stop-and-start rhythm, lackadaisical as an opium dream. But with Hank it was one of their songs, furious and crazed, and she seemed to glimpse him in pieces, clenched teeth and glossy eyes.

Afterward, he held her, still panting, and said, "Man, Lilly. Am I in love with you? What's happening?"

"You're in love with me in a way. But it's not a relationship way."

"You're the person who I'm closest to in the whole world."

"Me too," she said, staring straight into the crushed-velvet brown of his eyes.

"So why aren't we together?"

She shook her head. "Hell if I know."

"It's so fucked up," he said. "Here we are, lying around postcoitally, and it feels so safe. Like this is some new kind of relationship where you don't have to own the other person or get obsessed with them or hurt them. But if we were together for real, it would never be like this."

"Probably not." She sat up and snapped off the light. "We sure as hell weren't before. Remember the time I crashed your bike into that tree? I was bleeding all over and you were yelling at me." She laughed. "You were acting like I spazzed out and hit that tree on purpose."

She had curled against him and could feel him laugh a

little, too. "Well, you *were* riding no-handed on my brand-new bike," he said.

As she drifted off, she thought how strange it was. Right after the bike incident she had hated Hank the way she sometimes hated Dieter now, the way you can only hate someone you love. Why did it have to be like that, one person yelling and the other one bloody? A few minutes ago, grinding on top of Hank, she'd locked eyes with him; he hadn't looked back at her with the glommy gaze of a lover, but with the soft-focus, distracted eyes of a friend. This had been her first experience of a friend fuck, and she understood why people did it—slept with their exes. You rolled off the other person sweaty but poised, still yourself, safe.

Maybe it would be possible—she thought, almost asleep now—to invent some new kind of relationship without all the yelling and the blame, without the fear of being dumped. An extended friend fuck. In the morning, she thought, in the morning I'll invent it.

When they got back to Boston, she didn't want to go home. And so she didn't. She wandered down to the river and sat on a rock. Soon she'd have to go back to her apartment, and he'd be there, slumped over a book or scribbling down notes. She could feel the apartment, lurking beyond those trees across the river; evil vibes emanated from that direction. She dreaded the moment when he examined her face and said, "What's wrong with you? There's something you're not telling me."

Eventually she stood up. She found that, instead of crossing the bridge, she was walking in the opposite direction. She followed Memorial Drive and then slid through the gates of Harvard Stadium to cut across the fields toward Allston.

She felt so bruised by Dieter. He was always slipping away from her, into a book or a pouty mood. She'd been lonely for months now, she realized, because of the way he ignored her. What she needed was a boyfriend who was slavishly devoted to her. Or maybe, maybe what she needed was two boyfriends.

The idea was so brilliant that she stopped, surprised, right in the middle of the field. Two boyfriends! She closed her eyes and remembered how perfect it had been when she sat crammed on the sofa between Dieter and Hank. Dieter's hand had fondled her thigh; Hank's arm had wrapped around her shoulder. For a moment, it had been like she had a boyfriend with four arms and two heads, a boyfriend who could surround her in his flesh.

"Maybe there are some women who just need two men," she thought, and just naturally she began to turn it into a song. "Make me a man sandwich," she sang in her head, experimenting with different tunes. "Spread me on two slices," she tried. "It's one of my vices."

She kept on walking, across the field and into the neighborhood, as she sang the new song in her head. By the time she found herself standing in front of Hank's house, she'd finished it. She sat on the moldy sofa on his porch, took a napkin out of her purse, and wrote the whole song down.

She couldn't read music; she used her own system of symbols. When she was finished, she crammed the napkin back in her purse.

Then she slipped through the open door, said hi to Hank's housemates Eric and Hannah, went upstairs, and got into his empty bed. Just the way the sheets smelled—of all-American boy, of locker room—calmed her. She lay in that bed like it was some kind of womb.

She woke up when the door opened. "Lil," he said. "Hannah told me you were here. What's wrong?"

"Nothing," she said, but to her surprise she heard her voice crack.

He slid in next to her. "Oh man, it's my fault. We shouldn't have slept together." He held her in that way she loved, just on the verge of too tight. They started kissing. His mouth was like all the comfort food in the world: grits, white gravy, and sweet potato pie.

She pulled him down into that bed, a cocoon of warmth. "I wrote a song." She turned to him, under the white gloom of the sheet, and sang it.

"That's great. But why are you here? Did you just talk to Dieter?" Hank stroked hair, examined her face.

"No, I didn't go home."

"Are you scared to?"

"Yes." She sighed, her voice uncertain, as if she might cry.

"Maybe you shouldn't tell him. Look, we slipped up. It'll never happen again. Whatever. Right?" Hank sat up. "In fact, we shouldn't be doing this."

"I'm sorry," she said, pulling herself up too. "The whole

thing's so messed up. I don't know if I should even be with Dieter. I just want to stay here with you."

"I know, I know," he said, touching her arm. "But just go home now, okay?"

And so she went back to the apartment and Dieter didn't notice anything. Instead, he dragged her over to the sofa and started blabbing about the play he'd been asked to help write and the gossip he'd heard and the leak he'd fixed.

"Poor Dieter," she said, holding him. "You've been all cooped up here with no one to talk to, haven't you?"

"Yeah," he said, casting his eyes down.

She kissed him softly on the side of his head, the place that always smelled of gingerbread.

After that, the weirdest thing happened. Everything went back to normal. Dieter still hung out at Hank's house. She saw Hank at practice, and they argued about equipment and chord changes like always—nothing sexual. Sometimes Hank came over to their apartment to watch a video or lend Dieter a tool. And she could pretend, it was easy to pretend, that nothing had changed.

She and Hank slipped up a few times. One Sunday Lilly showed up at the Middle East for the *Sound* benefit. When she glanced across the room, she noticed Hank, leaning against a pillar, watching the band on stage. Suddenly she wanted him so bad she couldn't stand it. Not in a sexual way, really. She wanted him the way she craved hard liquor, cigarettes, pink cake, and coffee with clotted cream.

She'd sidled up and stared at him, not saying anything.

"Let's go for a walk," he said. And like she was in a dream, she followed him out the door, and before they'd even gone a block, they were making out against a wall. And then they were whizzing along on their bikes and falling into Hank's bed.

Still Dieter didn't notice. Just the opposite—things got easy with him, maybe because she let him alone now, didn't grab his book away so he'd listen, didn't harangue him, didn't try to get him to like her music, didn't nag him to go to shows with her.

"Hey, hon," she'd call. "Do we have any cereal?"

"I think we're out," he'd answer from the other room.

"Should I get some? What kind do you want?" And it was like that, all low-key negotiation, all breeziness.

And she told herself that soon she'd stop with Hank. That already she'd stopped. So she wasn't lying, really. There were just things that, for Dieter's own sake, she wouldn't tell him.

Who knows how long this might have lasted, if Lilly's coworker hadn't come into the café one morning with the new copy of *The Sound*. She grabbed Lilly's arm and said in a strained voice, "You better look at this."

Lilly took the smeary newsprint magazine, folded open to the offending page, and the first thing she saw was her name and Hank's in bold.

The gossip column read: "In the hey-we-want-our-money-back department, here's a scandalous tidbit: Every time the Exes get on stage, they tell us that—though their members used to pork each other—they're just one big happy platonic family now. Only one problem. The Exes aren't actually exes, if you believe the report of one of our spies. He says he saw **Lilly Major** and **Hank Alvey** getting *very* frisky with one another. Maybe they should be called the Frauds . . ."

Lilly looked up from the newsprint. The tables, the counters, the brick walls, everything around her seemed to be waiting for her explanation.

Shaz

Shaz slid through the door of Vile Vinyl and glanced around, almost hoping Hank wouldn't be there. Maybe it was his day off. She didn't see anyone in the store besides the slacker dude lounging behind the register.

She remembered when Hank used to stand up on that platform, behind the register. He'd looked just like that slacker dude back then—standing at the front of the store like he couldn't believe his luck at being picked to work at the best used-record store in town. She remembered that first time she talked to him, waiting in line with her CD so he could ring her up. When he caught sight of her, he'd started jiggling his pen. "You're Shazia Dohra." His voice had cracked. "I'm a big fan."

And now here she was almost two years later, scared of him. For months, she'd let Hank boss her around. He loaded her into the van like a piece of equipment; he scheduled her weekends full of gigs; he'd even started to tell her how her bass parts should sound. She'd tolerated it for a while, thinking things would get better. But she couldn't take it anymore.

Now—with a jab in her stomach—she realized he was here. He was at the other end of the store, leaning over a bin of CDs, expertly pinching labels out of a pricing gun. She wiped her hands on her jeans and walked toward him.

While he worked, Hank lectured some guy who slumped in a chair beside him—probably one of his groupies. Hank complained about it, how people glommed onto him these days. He and Lilly had become local celebrities—they'd gotten their picture in the *Globe* and been interviewed on WZBC and WMBR and even WFNX. The two of them were the famous faces from the Exes. Shaz and Walt were the back-up players, the anonymous ones. That was fine with Shaz.

"My favorite Boston punk band ever was the Girls," Hank was telling his groupie. "You should really check them out. Their stuff is on a few compilations."

"Hey there," Shaz called.

Hank turned around, blinked. "Wow. What brings you here?"

"I wanted to talk," she said. "Let's go somewhere, OK?"

"Sure," he said. "Just wait a sec." He swaggered through a door marked EMPLOYEES ONLY. After ten minutes or so, he emerged from the back room, shrugging on his jacket. "I don't care. Flush them down the toilet. Just get rid of them," he called over his shoulder to somebody she couldn't see. He was laughing still, from some gag they'd been playing back there. He turned toward her, seeming almost surprised that she was still waiting.

"Where do you want to go?" he said.

"Let's just sit on the stairs out front."

So they settled on the cold concrete of the stoop, Shaz hugging her legs, Hank sprawled out. It was a misty November evening; cars swept by, their tires hissing on the damp concrete.

"What's up?" Hank said. He was rolling a cigarette, using his jean-covered thigh as a work surface. When had he begun smoking? This must be part of the new, superstar Hank persona.

She pushed her hair back, then blurted out, "I don't want to mess things up for you guys. You've got to understand that."

He took a hit off the cigarette, making the tobacco sizzle, then leaned back against the rail, enjoying the smoke. "I don't get it. What's the problem?"

She swallowed. Her spit felt like acid. "I can't go on this tour," she said.

He didn't even register surprise. Instead, he sucked on the cigarette and quickly exhaled the smoke. "Okay, calm down. Tell me slowly."

She squirmed around on the cold concrete. A week ago, she'd come home and found a message from him on her machine, his voice loud with excitement. Bronco Records. Cut a CD. Go on a national tour. Advertising. Promotion. Studio time. The words had leaped out at her; his prerecorded voice rattling on and on. "You better get ready now," the voice had said, and then it listed its instructions for her—she would need to take at least a month off from work in March and could she be at a photo shoot next Thursday? Shaz had hunched over the answering machine and finally clicked off Hank's voice in midsentence. Standing there in the sudden silence of her apartment, she had a panicky feeling that she'd lost control, that her own fate was a recorded message she could not erase or turn off.

Now she caught Hank's eye. "It's just . . . ," she began. "I never thought any of this would happen. I never wanted to be in some big indie band. I thought this was just for fun."

"You don't want to be in a big indie band." He repeated this back to her like she was retarded. "So why the hell have we been working our butts off all this time? We might be able to quit our day jobs eventually."

She shifted her weight, not sure how to explain it. Whenever she tried to talk to Hank these days, everything she said sounded dumb. "Look," she tried. "Even if I could quit my job, I wouldn't want to."

"Why not?" He flicked his cigarette away. "This is so frustrating. You're incredibly talented, Shaz. You deserve to turn pro."

"I'm not that good."

"Yes you are. You're better than I'll ever be. And you're just going to piss that away so you can keep some dumb-ass job? I mean, what do you even do? You put dicks on cakes."

She made a motion, like she was about to leave.

"I'm sorry," he said, waving his hand for her to stay.

"That was stupid." Underneath that swagger and cool, underneath the scuffed leather coat, he was fond of her—she knew that. Underneath, maybe he was the same old Hank. "It just . . . I guess it hurts my feelings." His voice sounded thin and high. "I thought this band meant a lot to you."

She tilted her head toward him. "It does. But you're asking me to give up everything else, the whole rest of my life."

"No I'm not. Where did you get that idea?"

She was silent for a moment, searching for words. "If I go on the tour with you guys, that's six weeks at least. And then, if we're going to be a real indie band, that's pretty much a full-time thing. I'd be out of town half the year."

"Half the year if we're lucky. But that's not so bad. That's not your whole life."

She stared at him. "Yes it is. What about those guys like Ray and Greg? They're complete alcoholics. All those guys who tour a lot, you've seen how messed up they get."

"Oh, Shaz, come on. They were already like that."

She shook her head. It was hopeless, trying to explain it to him. "Anyway, you know how I hate being stuck in that van. I don't want to do that every day for months and months."

Suddenly Hank seemed to crumble. He rubbed his face, like he was trying to wake up. "I had a feeling something like this was going to happen. Not you—I didn't know it would be you—but I knew something would screw up."

"It's not screwed up," she said. "You can easily get someone else. There are lots of bass players around." She knew a couple of different bands that had gone on tour with some musician they picked up at the last minute; it happened pretty often.

"You've been with us for a year and a half or something, and now you're just going to walk out?"

She drew in her breath sharply. "Look, I'm sorry. I really am, Hank. I didn't think it would be such a big deal."

"Of course it is. This totally shits."

"Well, it's just . . . How do you think I feel? All of a sudden I find out there's this contract and this tour. You never even told me you were sending our demo tape to Bronco."

"Don't give me that. You knew, Shaz. Why are you screwing me over like this?" he said, sounding like he was about to cry. "Oh, man, I can't believe this is happening."

She could smell the nervous sweat on him.

"I'm sorry," she said again, uselessly. "I should have quit a long time ago. We should have talked."

"No kidding." His voice cracked.

"I just didn't know it would be such a big deal. I mean, I never thought of myself as a real member of the band. The Exes is you and Lilly. It's your thing."

"I'm sorry you feel that way," he said quietly. "I see it now, though. You told me a long time ago that you didn't want to get too involved." He shook his head. "I didn't believe you. I thought once we got a contract and stuff you'd change your mind."

She put her arm around his bent back, leaned her face against the cracked leather of his jacket. It was weird touching Hank; she'd never done it before. "Seriously, you don't need me," she said. "You can get that guy Chet to go."

"I don't want to talk about it anymore," he said. Slowly, he stood up, turned around, and disappeared behind the dark glass of the door.

Shaz sat there for a while, her butt freezing on the concrete, her fists balled up in the pockets of her jacket. Finally she stood up and started on the long walk home. As she strode over the Mass. Ave. bridge, the sharp wind turned her face into a circle of cold, and the water heaved underneath her. On the Cambridge side, there was a weird reek to the air, and she realized it must be the Necco factory, the place where they made those candy hearts for Valentine's Day. The air was just like those hearts: chemical and sweet. This smell was the smell of something else, too, something that made her breath shallow with excitement. She slowed her walk, tried to catch a whiff again to figure out what it reminded her of. Then it hit her.

When you peeled off the shrink-wrap from a new CD, when you snapped open the case for the first time, this was the odor that wafted up—sugar dissolved in brake fluid, honey mixed with Drano, chocolate cake slathered with nonoxynol-9. She loved that new-CD smell; she loved lifting the CD out with her fingertips and setting it on its little throne; she loved the second of silence while you waited, and then the notes thundering out of the speakers.

The Cambridge night smelled of new CDs and it made her high the way the best songs did—like sugar dissolved in brake fluid, like an acid trip coming on, like Mickey when she was in love with him. For a moment she wanted to risk everything. She wanted to go on tour with the Exes just to keep feeling this high, this skittery crazed mania; she wanted to be on a stage so she could jump into the mosh pit and fly into the churning bodies to see who would catch her. She wanted to step out of her own skin and into something else.

But you can't build a life around whatever crazy impulse hits you. She'd learned that much at least. After all the shit she'd been through, she'd finally achieved a quiet kind of happiness. She'd found a truth she could curl around, the way your hand curls around a worry bead. Its polished surface winked with light, always there at her center. She wouldn't lose it. She was determined not to lose it this time.

Three years ago, she played bass for Girl Power. They sucked. Shaz was the only one who knew how to tune her guitar. It didn't matter. Girl Power wore great costumes and go-go danced around the stage. They were the house band in this gay-girl bar, Amelia's, and just being a woman on stage hammering on an electric guitar was enough. The audience loved you no matter what.

Shaz would show up at the last minute for those gigs, threading her way through the crowd so she could jump right up on stage and plug in her bass. "Hey, you made it," her bandmates would exclaim, surprised and delighted, as if she were an unexpected guest at a party. The room was stuffy with the smell of patchouli; the women in the audience stood close, chatting with each other. They danced with wide hips and big arms, sweating profusely. When Girl Power finished their set, Shaz would climb back down to the floor and into that swirl of tits and painted mouths to find Kate, her girlfriend at the time, a small, dark woman who worked her butt off running a feminist bookstore. The job had given Kate circles under her eyes and turned her into a compulsive pot smoker. But still, there she was waiting for Shaz after the show, stroking her hair, saying, "That made my day. You guys are so great."

And they'd sit at a table with their friends, listening to the house sound, songs that made Shaz wince—the Indigo Girls, Holly Near, Michelle Shocked. Women's music. Most of it was lame. But still, she'd grown to love those songs just because they were familiar. They were as comfortable as the old flannel shirt you wore when you felt sick.

The whole dyke scene was like that. It was you in your apartment, lip-synching to a song you knew wasn't cool. It was you as a twelve-year-old girl, dressed up like one of the guys in the Knack with a sock stuffed in your pants. It was sick days and snow days and notes from your mother saying you couldn't play volleyball during Ramadan.

In a weird way, it even *was* your mother—or at least, your mother on those afternoons when the Ladies of Islam came over. They arrived in their stiffly pressed American dresses and their *shalwar kameezes* to discuss the Koran. Or so they said when the fathers asked.

Shaz and her brother couldn't wait for the Ladies of Islam days, because that's when all rules went out the window.

She and her brother stuffed leftover cake in their mouths and bumped down the stairs on their butts. The mothers in the living room never noticed. They gorged on cake and *gulab jamuns,* and sometimes erupted into giggles all at once, like the laugh track to a sitcom. Their eyes squinted into the shape of the lemon rinds next to their tea, their earrings were like candy.

When she was very young—five or six—Shaz had already decided to live in the country of women. She knew such a place existed because her mother had told her. "You belong to two countries," her mother said, and Shaz didn't have to ask what they were. There was the country where men went, a place full of offices where the air always smelled like a Xerox machine, and the country of women, a shuttered suburban house where you could binge on cake and laugh until your stomach hurt.

And here, here in Amelia's on Sunday nights, she had found her country. The fat women with pierced tongues would be hanging out by the bar, guffawing with wide open faces; the slick-haired baby dykes would be crammed around tables, talking furiously; the hard-looking old hippies would be playing pool. In here, you forgot that Bush was president—and when you remembered, it all seemed like a big joke. "A bush in the White House!" You laughed, and ever after you couldn't help thinking of the president as a withered-up vagina.

The country of women—it wasn't perfect, but Shaz was happy here. Or at least she was until the night Mickey came into Amelia's.

She'd just played a set with Girl Power and was climbing down from the stage to find her coat. That's when she caught sight of him. At first she thought he was a big woman in drag. She just couldn't believe a man had found his way into Amelia's and had staked out his own table, his legs stretched out unapologetically in front of him. He wore a trench coat and his wide curly hair erupted over the collar. The moment she saw him, she knew he'd come here for her.

"Excuse me. Shazia? Sorry to bother you," he said, catching her eye.

"What?" She came over to his table. "Do I know you?"

"No, no. I've heard of you, though," he said. "I'm putting together a project, and I wonder if you'd be interested in it." He reached into his coat pocket and withdrew a pack of foreign-looking unfiltered cigarettes. Then he motioned to the seat beside him.

She slid into it, watching as he tamped down the end of his cigarette. "Oh, how rude of me," he said, and held out the pack, shaking it so that one cigarette slid toward her.

"No thanks," she said.

"Can I buy you a drink?" He held one hand in the air to flag down a nonexistent waiter, then shook his head in pretend exasperation. "I'll be back in a minute. What will you have?"

She hesitated a moment, sensing that this decision mattered—that she could prove her coolness by picking the right drink. No, it was more than that. She didn't want to break the spell he'd cast. He carried his atmosphere around with him—a Vegas-in-the-fifties, brush-on-snare-drum masculine fabulousness. She had forgotten this about men: the way some of them seemed to star in their own private movies.

"A Cosmopolitan," she said finally.

He nodded in approval, disappeared, and a few minutes later came back with two neat drinks.

"I'll be blunt," he said, as he sat down. "You're way too good to be in that dreadful band. I came here tonight only because I heard about you. Somebody told me that there was this awful all-women band that had one of the best bass players around."

"Can I just say that my band is not awful?" Shaz leaned toward him. "People like us. Look at this crowd."

"All right, fine. Let's not argue. Let's just say you might want to play with people who are a little more your speed. Tell me," he said, taking a long drag on his cigarette, "where did you learn to play like that?"

She shrugged, squirmed around in her chair. "I don't know. When puberty hit, I'd spend hours in my room, stoned, cross-legged on my Snoopy quilt, playing my brother's guitar. The typical teenage thing. I played along with records. It was my way of dealing."

He was leaning forward, listening intently. It kind of creeped her out. She watched his fingers caressing the cigarette. "Whatever," she said. "It was the same thing everyone went through."

"Not me. I had zero attention span as a kid. I've been trying to make up for it ever since." He knocked back the rest of his drink.

"What do you play?"

He shrugged. "Whatever I need to. I'm more of a producer, really. The shadowy Phil Spector–like presence. As I said, right now I'm putting a group of musicians together."

"So"—she wrinkled her forehead—"are you looking for someone to join your band, or just help out on a few tracks? I don't get it."

"I can't explain it here," he said, gesturing around the room, where women were saying their goodbyes and finishing up their drinks. Was he afraid that someone might overhear them and steal his ideas? Or did he mean that the atmosphere was all wrong? "Let me give you this," he said, reaching into his coat pocket. "My card." He left it on the table and disappeared in a swirl of gabardine, leaving behind a scent of Turkish tobacco.

She picked up the card and studied it. "Golden Arm Recording Studio," it said in embossed script. "We offer vintage sound equipment and old-fashioned know-how. Mick Sloan, proprietor."

She was still staring at the card when her bandmate Laurie plopped down into the chair he'd just left. "Let me see." Laurie took the card and studied it. "Hmmm. That guy— what a trip. I can't believe he came in here."

"You know him?"

"Not really. I've had him pointed out to me at parties. Some people think he's a genius and some people think he's full of shit. My opinion? It's usually a little of both. Shit and genius, all mixed together."

"He wants me to work on some musical project with

him, but I don't trust him," Shaz said. "I'm not going to call him."

And she didn't. But a few weeks later, she was walking down Mass. Ave. when he appeared right in front of her—he'd just come out of a store—and she nearly collided with him. Mickey touched her shoulder for a second. "Whoa," he said. "What's the hurry?" It was almost as if he'd arranged to be there. Maybe he had. Once you knew Mickey for a while, you realized that his life had been a long succession of lucky breaks and charmed coincidences.

"Oh, sorry," she said. "I didn't see you."

"Listen. I need to talk to you," he said. "What are you doing right now?"

"Now? Walking home."

"Come with me," he said, with such urgency she didn't question it. And soon, they sat in his recording studio, an old factory loft in East Cambridge. He lived in the back; the front was like a cavern, with a mixing board against one wall, and rows of old-fashioned microphones, tube amps, and reel-to-reel tapes.

He picked out a sleek Rickenbacker and handed it to her. "I'm going to play some recordings for you. You just improvise along, okay?" he said. "Then we'll see what you can do."

"Look, don't put me on the spot," she said. "I didn't agree to audition for you."

"I'm not auditioning you. This is just for fun." He popped a tape into the control board of his sound system. Some kind of funk-oriented jazz swelled out of the speakers. "You like this?" he asked.

"It's okay." She began jamming along with it, quietly at first. But soon she sort of forgot he was there, and she began doing what came naturally, popping the strings and playing little countermelodies.

Mickey put in another tape, and another. Occasionally he would suggest something: "Do that one again," he might say, "and I'll hook you up to this effects box. It's going to make you sound high and whiny, kind of like one of those horns the snake charmers use. Try using some minor progressions."

She'd do what he said, and sometimes he'd get all excited and say, "Yes, perfect." Other times he'd say, "Yeah, that's good, but try to make it sound more like this." Then he'd pull out another tape and play it for her. Mostly the music was new to her, and she listened with her eyes closed, intent, as if she could soak up the unfamiliar sound through her skin.

After an hour or so, they were talking in half sentences. "The mournful, dirge thing. Yeah," he'd say.

"Shorter," she'd answer.

She'd never experienced this before—the feeling of being perfectly in sync with another musician. It was almost as if Mickey sat inside her brain with her, hearing the way she heard, anticipating her decisions.

When she glanced at her watch, it was much later than she thought. "Oh crap," she said. "I've got to go."

He called her later that night. "I hope we can work together. You're just what I'm looking for."

"Yeah, okay, maybe," she said. "I mean, what about the

other people you've got? Don't you have three other guys in your band, or whatever it is? I should try jamming with them."

"Absolutely," he said. "But maybe not yet. I've thought a lot about this. You're much better in the studio, much more comfortable playing with tapes, because you learned how to play from records when you were a kid. The only live musicians you've worked with weren't very good. So I thought that the best thing was to get you to improvise along with recordings for a while. Work with you that way first."

"Yeah," she said. "It is easier to play along with a tape. But that's not really the point, is it? I need to get better at working with real people."

"I have this theory—maybe you've chosen to play with amateurs because you're afraid of being with talented musicians," he said.

"Look, they're my friends—that's why I play with them. Not because I'm afraid of anything." She was annoyed at the way he was psychoanalyzing her. And yet she was kind of intrigued, too. No one had ever bothered to figure out how she would play her best. No one had ever constructed a theory about her.

A week later, she went to his loft again. They did pretty much the same thing—Mickey put on tapes, she jammed, and he made suggestions. Sometimes he picked up a guitar or a keyboard and put in a few fills himself; he was an okay musician, but she could tell he was better at figuring out what other people should do. After a few hours of intense jamming, Shaz leaned back in her chair and said, "Uggh, I'm worn out."

"Yeah, I am too. My lord, happy hour has come and gone and we didn't even notice. Listen, I'm going to have a dry martini." He got up, said over his shoulder, "What do you want? Martini?"

She followed him into the apartment part of his loft. They sat at a high table in what was more or less the kitchen—it was hard to tell where the rooms began and ended because the place had no walls. His vintage refrigerator hummed next to a spare, 1950s couch; the bathtub sat out in plain view, its plumbing around it like a delicate scaffolding.

He expertly mixed a martini for her, fishing an olive out of the jar with a swizzle stick. After he'd set the drink in front of her, he began asking questions in that professional voice, as if he were gathering information for some dossier. Was she Indian? No? Pakistani? Had she ever been there? Did she see much of her family now?

She picked up her drink, answering his questions in a halfhearted way as she wandered around the apartment. While she talked, she examined the stuff on his countertop and looked through his cabinets. Once in a while, she'd shoot back a question at him: "What's in here? What's this?"

And so they interrogated each other. After his first martini, Mickey stopped asking her about her family and got down to the serious shit. "So, if you were in Girl Power," he said, "I assume you're gay. Forgive me for saying so, but you don't seem gay."

She didn't know how to answer. Kate was officially her girlfriend, but after a year together, their relationship had mutated into something halfway between lovers and best friends. They both got laid by guys now and then. Neither of them were jealous of each other's escapades in boyland. Why be jealous? The last time Shaz was with a guy, the best part of it was the next morning, when she gossiped about it with Kate. "He wanted to do it in the shower," she confided over the phone. "It was fun, but eventually I had to break it to him that soap really stings."

Now Shaz paused a minute in front of Mickey's refrigerator, touching the magnets. She couldn't figure out how to explain it. Finally she said, "I'm bi, and I have a girlfriend." She let all the rest of it hang in the air.

"Hmm, you're bi," Mickey said, leaning back in his chair and taking a drag off his cigarette. "Tell me—and you don't have to answer this if you're sick of people asking—but tell me: What's the difference between having sex with men and women?"

"I don't know how to describe it, really," she said, pausing a moment. "I'll tell you one thing. It's a lot easier to be straight than gay. There are more people to choose from."

"But you don't like to do things the easy way, is that it?" he said, lifting one eyebrow. Somehow it was a proposition.

"I guess not." Now she stopped in front of the stereo and flipped through his records.

He sat forward in his chair, planting one foot on each side of her. She picked up a record to look at its liner notes.

He said, "Perez Prado. Have you heard him?"

"No." She felt herself tensing up. Mickey was leaning in toward her. He wasn't actually that close—his head was maybe a foot away from hers. But it was close enough. She was allowing him to enter her space. She felt as if he were pressed up against her back.

It was guys—more than women—who came onto you this way. There was a certain kind of guy who would decide that, just because he liked you, you belonged to him. She had a weakness for this kind. A few months ago, she'd been sleeping with a guy named Sanjeev. With his British-school accent, his button-down shirts, and those perfectly trimmed fingernails, he reminded her of the men from her childhood. They had been as vain and as charming as movie stars, and they liked to lecture you about the foolishness of your liberal ideas.

She first met Sanjeev when he sidled up to her at a party and told her she would look beautiful if only she wore a dress instead of those jeans; tomorrow he was taking her shopping.

"How about I buy you a dress?" she'd said. "You'd look better in it than me." Their brief fling had been like a wrestling match where she won every round.

Mickey reminded her of Sanjeev; he had that seductively irritating quality about him, like an itchy scab that you can't stop picking at. But Mickey was more dangerous. He didn't care about getting laid, or about impressing her with his taste, not exactly. He wanted something more precious from her, something she couldn't have named if she tried. She had a dizzying sense that she had lost control of the situation.

Now, for lack of anything better to do, she slid the LP out of its sleeve. "Should I put this on?"

"Yeah, I think you'll dig it," he said, still close behind her.

"Okay, I'll put it on," she said, but instead of leaning toward the stereo she collapsed against his leg. "I—that martini was really strong, wasn't it?"

"Not especially." He took a drag off his cigarette, seeming not to notice how she had fallen against him.

"I guess I'm just worn out." She shifted her weight, to move away from him.

He put his hand on her shoulder. "Stay," he said. And then she heard him take another drag on his cigarette.

"I think I'm falling in love with you," he said flatly.

"What?" She pulled away. She felt like she'd just inhaled nitrous oxide, or like she was floating in the airless atmosphere of the moon. "That's crazy. You don't know me."

"Do you have to know someone to fall in love with them?"

"Yes," she said.

"I think most people fall in love with strangers. That's why they came up with the metaphor of Cupid's arrows. Something that hits you in the chest like an arrow, from out of nowhere."

"Is that how you feel now?" She had adopted the same ultrarational tone he used.

"It's never been like this before," he said. "Whenever I meet a musician I want to work with, I get really excited. I suppose it's like falling in love, in a platonic way—it's seeing all the potential of this person. But so far I've only experienced that with men, never a woman. You—you're the first one. I don't know what it means."

"It sounds like you just want to work with me. Like it's not sexual," she said.

He chortled. "I assure you, it is sexual."

She stood up and moved away from him to lean against the bar. "This is freaking me out."

"I'm sorry," he said, sucking on the cigarette again.

She couldn't figure out what he was up to—why he sat there like a blob and at the same time insisted he was in love with her. She kept asking him questions about how he felt and he'd try to explain it. She found herself moving closer to him as they talked, until finally she was standing beside his chair.

"Forgive me for saying this," he was telling her, "I know it's sexist, but the strange thing about you is that you play bass like a man. All the women bass players I've heard, they're afraid to improvise. They just want to make sure they're doing everything right. But you—"

She leaned over, swiped the hair out of his face, and pushed her tongue into his mouth. He tasted like gin, but he smelled of something else—a sweet, almondy odor mixed with the stench of cigarettes. His smell acted on her like a drug. She knew she would never get enough. She angled her tongue in deep against the ridged roof of his mouth. For one intoxicating moment, she imagined her tongue had turned into a dick, and she was fucking him.

He pulled away. "No," he said. "Stop. I want to kiss you, but not like that."

"What?" she said, hurt. "What's wrong?"

"I just—You weren't there with me. You weren't responding to me."

She turned her head away, blinking. She felt like she used to back in high school, when she tried to pick up guys and scared them off instead—she suddenly pictured herself as desperate and way too horny and sloppy drunk. She hadn't felt this awkward in a long time. She glanced back at him. "Well, I was into it. But never mind."

"All right. Don't get mad now," he said. "Come here." He took her arm and guided her toward him, kissed her delicately. She wanted to be greedy, to suck the air out of him, but she forced herself to do it his way.

"Touch me gently," he said. And it was like their jam session just a few hours before—he taught and she tried to follow along. No, it wasn't like that. Because with the music there'd been a kind of equality: he knew how to put together a song, but she had better chops. With sex, though, it all had to be his way.

"Calm down," he said, when they were lying on his bed. "Relax." She did as she was told. His smell, his black eyes, his womanish skin—it was like some kind of food she'd been craving all her life. He guided her until she lay on her back with her knees bent. "Like this," he said.

She had an odd and unfamiliar feeling of giving herself

up to someone. Her own hands seemed far away, like they didn't belong to her. The word "missionary" flashed in her mind, and suddenly she understood it, why they called it that.

He fell asleep and she stayed awake, gazing around his room. Her own shirt, in a rumpled heap on the floor, glowed in the moonlight like a silver sculpture. A chair in the corner sat plumply silent. All the objects in the room seemed like they were meditating. Her mind suddenly cleared, and she had a sense of comradeship with these silent objects. She understood everything now: Mickey wanted to invade her brain. He had planned to move into the quiet room she kept inside her head, the room with the locked door where only she could go. She wouldn't let him.

First thing, she'd go and tell Kate. She began composing the story about Mickey, figuring out what she would say. "He's one of those audiophile guys, so of course we had to listen to exactly the right music," she would tell Kate. "I was pretty turned on by him. Too bad he would only agree to vanilla sex. Missionary position."

But the next day she didn't even mention Mickey. Maybe it was because Kate showed up at a bad time. Shaz was making up a batch of pink chocolate to put into the penis molds, her hands all covered with goop, when she heard the doorbells jingle and a voice called, "Hey there, Sweetie."

At the sound of Kate's voice, Shaz felt a peculiar panic. She wiped her hands and went out to the front. "Hi," she said. "How did it go with Susie Bright? Did you ever reach her?"

"I left a message with her publicist. I don't know. It looks kind of grim." Kate was always trying to get sex experts to lead workshops at her store.

"I'm really hot and annoyed," Shaz said. "I've got to make at least fifty pink penises today. I don't mind doing the black ones because then you can use regular chocolate, but I hate the white chocolate we've got. It's so greasy."

"Well, tell me how the audition went. Weren't you going to try out for some band last night?"

Shaz felt her face flush. She turned away. "Yeah," she said, pretending to check on one of the trays. "It was good. I might join." She willed herself to turn around, tell Kate what happened. But already it was too late. She should have said something the minute Kate walked in the store. "I got laid last night," she might have put it, and then launched into her story. But for some reason, she felt suddenly shy.

Two days later, Shaz did lie. Kate called, wanting her to spend the night, and the excuse just poured out of Shaz's mouth. "I'm going to practice with this new band tonight," she said. "I won't be finished till late."

After she hung up, she felt like a total creep. She'd never lied to Kate before. She did it with other lovers occasionally —kept them fenced off from the rest of her life, made polite excuses. It was different with Kate. Or supposed to be different anyway—but Shaz had just begun to understand that there had always been parts of herself she'd been afraid to show Kate, tide pools and murky puddles of unfeminist feelings.

As it turned out, Walt was the person she told first. They

were hanging out at Dell's Diner, and he was ranting about some crackpot project. If she'd been less obsessed with Mickey at the time, she might have figured out that Walt was going nuts—that he would check himself into a loony bin less than a month later. She knew Walt had been staying up late in jags, working in the lab trying to grow proteins in petri dishes, trying to coax the cells into multiplying and forming delicate crystals. Now he'd decided that songs could be grown the same way—that if you fed a few notes and rhythm sequences into a computer, the song would form all by itself, like something in a petri dish.

Of course Shaz agreed to help him with this insane project. She had this persistent feeling that she owed Walt; no matter how many favors she did for him, she never paid off the debt. He'd moved to Boston first; when she decided to come out here, she'd crashed at his place—or in his bed, to be more specific. Walt lent her money, introduced her around, helped her get a job. He was like that—incredibly kind in his own ground-control-to-Major-Tom kind of way.

After a few months, she found her own place and paid him back. Without having to discuss it, they stopped sleeping together. The thing was, she couldn't really imagine Walt as a real boyfriend. Especially not back then.

He used to be so uptight. When you saw past his shaggy hair and ripped shirts, you realized he was like a dad from an old sitcom, one of those guys who lurks in his study until there's trouble with the kids. Walt would be hunched over his four-track all day, completely ignoring her; but then, if she got upset, he'd suddenly try to click into emotional mode, nodding at everything she said, staring into her eyes. It was like he'd learned how to be human by watching TV.

For a while, she tried to break through to whatever was going on inside Walt. Sometimes she'd poke him until he said, "Quit it." Sometimes she'd ask him the kind of questions he hated, like "What's your bizarre-est sexual fantasy?" When she asked him that, he had scrunched up his face as if he were thinking hard, then he finally said, "I don't really have any." What could you do with that?

So obviously Walt wasn't the best person to confide in, especially that day in Dell's Diner, when he was starting to lose it. But in the throes of her obsession with Mickey, she didn't care; she hardly noticed poor Walt. She felt so full, so full of things to say, she might explode. One minute she was listening to Walt explain how a choruser box worked, and the next minute she heard herself start blabbing about Mickey. She was leaning over the table toward Walt, waving her hands around. She was saying, "At first, I was just going to have a fling with him. But then he called me on it. He said I keep myself hidden, emotionally. I resisted for a while, and then suddenly I realized he was right. So for the first time in my life I'm doing it; I'm letting myself fall in love all the way. I'm losing myself."

Walt was staring at her blankly. "I only care about what's good for him," she said, and then laughed self-consciously. "I don't know. Is that weird?"

Walt bit the side of his lip, something he did when he

was worried about you, or maybe when he was pretending to be worried about you. "That sounds kind of dangerous, actually."

"No, no, it's great. Mickey says that I've always been too afraid to really commit. I was always so chickenshit before. So self-involved."

"It's just . . ." Walt was silent a moment. "I guess that's great. Congratulations."

"What? Tell me, what are you thinking?"

"Well, it sounds like you're happy. But it's this evangelistic happiness, like you need to convince me of something because you're not really convinced yourself."

"I do?" Her voice cracked.

"This reminds me of something I just read about," Walt went on. "Did you know there's a specific psychological phenomenon that happens when people become born-again Christians? First of all, they distance themselves from their own past. They hate their pre-born-again selves. It's because their shift in belief systems is so extreme that they can't integrate their past and present selves."

She wanted to say, "You don't even get it, do you? You've never been in love like this," but she managed to keep her mouth shut. She gulped a mouthful of her wheatgrass juice and then meditatively wiped at the beads of water on the glass. Finally she spoke, slowly: "I don't exactly hate my old self. I'm just frustrated that I wasted so much time." She looked up. His forehead was wrinkled. "Whatever," she said. "This is a boring topic. You wanted to talk about your thing, right?"

What was the point in trying to make poor Walt understand? She gave up, though there was still so much she
wanted to say about Mickey. She wanted somebody to understand how amazing all this was, the way she had been
like a rosebud—closed and bullet-shaped—and suddenly
she had bloomed, her petals arching out, aching open toward the light.

She wanted somebody to know how she felt whenever she
walked into that hallway with its three battered mailboxes
and got her first hit of the smell of Mickey's apartment,
stale cigarette smoke mixed with the burnt-dust odor that
electronic equipment gives off. And then, how she felt
when she jogged up his stairs, how it reminded her of
climbing a scale until you reach the highest note, a soprano
moan that pierces your body like knives, so beautiful it
hurts.

Inside Mickey's studio, it was like being stuck on the
peak of that note for hours. The sun shivered on the wood
floor in the morning. The coffee seemed to come apart in
her mouth, separating into all its tastes—smoke and moss
and chocolate and blood. And Mickey himself lived at the
highest pitch all the time. Once he pulled her onto the bed
and just stared into her eyes. "I want to know you," he said.
"I'm going to look at you until I see you. Because you hide
from me, Shaz."

She laughed and tried to turn it into a joke, but he got all
annoyed. "I'm serious," he said. Eventually she went along
with it and stared back at him, into those hazel eyes,
muddy water where the dirt would never settle. She and

Mickey ended up lying on his bed, just staring, for seven hours straight. The weirdest part was that she never got bored, that whole time. In the end, it was the intensity that had bugged her. She'd finally jumped up and said, "This is going to drive me insane. I feel like I'm going insane."

Walt wouldn't have believed her if she told him about the staring. "For seven hours?" he might have said. "Are you sure it was seven hours? Maybe you fell asleep."

And Kate—if Kate ever heard about the staring, she'd burst out laughing.

When you got down to it, that was the real reason Shaz didn't want to tell Kate. It wasn't the jealousy factor she was afraid of, it was the when-worlds-collide factor. Every cool thing about Mickey would sound stupid if you tried to explain it to Kate.

"I don't think we should sleep together anymore." That's how Shaz put it when she finally got up the nerve to tell Kate. "I met a guy, and it's turning serious. But I don't want to lose you, Kate."

"Oh." Kate had been leaning over to touch Shaz's face, and now she landed in a chair with a little huff. "I knew something was up. We've hardly seen each other lately."

"Yeah, I know. I'm sorry. I should have told you a while ago, but, you know . . . Listen, you're my best friend, and for a long time, I thought that was what I wanted. But now, with this guy, I'm experiencing this other kind of love. It's like all the cheesy romantic movies."

Kate hugged her. "That's great," she said breathlessly. "I mean it." Already she held Shaz differently from how she used to; now her arms were spindly and loose around Shaz's neck. "Actually, to be honest, I feel shitty. But I'll get over it."

Of course, Kate wanted to know all about him.

"Oh, he's in that band I've been working with." Shaz let her voice trail off. She'd decided to be vague about Mickey, make him sound like some inoffensive musician guy.

Kate kept trying to pry. Eventually, she laughed. "You're not going to tell me anything, are you? I guess I'll have to check out this boy for myself."

And that was just the problem. Kate would want to meet Mickey as soon as possible. She would want to get drunk with him and talk late into the night, until jealousy melted into friendship; she would expect to drop by his place any time she needed to see Shaz; she'd think nothing of calling up and saying stuff like, "Hey you guys, I'm leaving town for a few days. Do you want to use my waterbed?" Kate thought of Shaz as family, and any serious boyfriend of hers would become family too.

When Shaz tried to explain this to Mickey, he hunched over in his favorite chair, stiffening whenever she tried to touch him. "You've been leaving me and going to her for months," he said. "And now I'm supposed to act like it's no big deal?"

"Come on, she just wants to keep things from getting weird," Shaz pleaded. "I mean, we're probably going to see her at a party or something anyway."

A few weeks later, he gave in. Kate dropped by his loft, bringing wine. That was her first infraction.

"Hmmm, *pink wine*," Mickey said. "I suppose we ought to *chill* it." This was a perfectly normal thing to say, but Shaz, picking up the sarcasm in his voice, knew he'd already classified her as a zinfandel drinker, a person who listened to world music, a backrub-giver, a wearer of baggy cotton clothing—a representative of all the things he sneered at.

You got used to this when you were around Mickey—his rules for living. He refused to drink beer or wine. In every thrift shop, he hunted out cardigan sweaters, especially the kind for golfers; he wouldn't wear a pullover. He despised Canadians; he obsessed about Japanese pop stars. It seemed completely arbitrary, the things Mickey had chosen to love, and Shaz often wondered how she'd become one of them—sometimes she felt like she'd been picked to be a member of an ultra-exclusive club.

Of course, Kate didn't care for clubs. She perched uncomfortably on one of Mickey's vintage chrome stools, gazing around the loft. There was so much Kate didn't approve of.

The band, for instance. Kate had been devastated when Shaz quit Girl Power. "Can't you be in two bands at once?" she'd pleaded. "They're your friends, Shaz. I've never seen you happier than when you were up there with them."

"I'm just tired of being the only one who can play my instrument," Shaz had said. "And now, in Sluggo, I'm learning so much."

"Oh, come on. Sluggo may be talented, but are they ever going to make bras out of Spam and parade through the streets?" That's what Girl Power did last year for the Pride march, and Shaz couldn't help laughing a little when Kate reminded her. But at the same time, she was annoyed at the way Kate wanted to stay forever in that one moment, marching down Boylston Street with two slabs of processed meat on her chest. It was a good moment, but it was over now.

How would she make Kate understand how Mickey had changed her? How could she make Kate understand any of the things she loved about Mickey? And now here Kate sat, gazing around at the mint-condition cocktail glasses and the framed picture of slit-eyed Betty Page in a leopard-skin bikini.

Kate didn't approve, but she was trying to be pleasant. She was drinking his martini. She was leaning toward him. "So you run a studio in here, and then—do you have another job, too?" she asked.

"Are you kidding?" Mickey said. "Usually it takes three people to do what I'm doing all alone. Right now, I'm producing a solo project for Ida Beam."

"Oh really?" Kate said, as if the name meant something to her. Shaz could hardly bear to listen. They were the two people she loved most, and they'd never get along.

When Kate finally left, Mickey paced back and forth. "Goddess worship and sex camps." He went over to the window and lit up a cigarette. "I just don't get it, Shaz. How could you put up with all that New Age crap? I mean, it's hard to imagine you were ever with her."

Shaz shook her head. "I'm still *with her.*" She was annoyed at how he insisted on turning everything into couples. "At this point, Kate's like family."

Mickey was flipping through the LPs. He did this whenever they began to have an argument. Now he held a record up to the light, searching it for scratches and dust. "It just seems backward, Shaz. I mean, Kate's like family. Walt's like family. You're always saying that about your old lovers. But what about your real family? You're barely in touch with them."

She felt tears well up in her eyes. How did he always manage to hit her where it hurt? "That's not fair. I talk to my mom a lot. But, you know, you have it easy. If you were gay, your parents would be fine with it. I mean, my mom's great, but she's still a Muslim, and there's just certain things she wouldn't be able to handle . . ."

"Like what?" he said, turning to her, his face crumpled with hurt. "That you're gay? Are you gay, Shaz?"

"I just . . ." She didn't know where to begin. "If I tell her about you, she'll assume we're getting married. She'll start, like, naming her grandchildren."

"Is it so impossible that we might get married and have kids?"

In the first few weeks they were together, Mickey kept asking her if she would stay with him forever. She would laugh it off and say, "How am I supposed to know?" She'd been sleeping with Kate then, which was probably what made Mickey so possessive. But lately he'd eased up. "Are you still on that marriage kick?" she asked.

"I don't know." He got up to turn the record over. Carefully, he lowered the needle onto the turntable. He always performed this task like some kind of religious ceremony, silent while the first notes of music swelled up. "I'm not so sure anymore."

"You're not?" she whispered. This was the last thing she expected him to say. She'd always laughed off his proposals, and yet it was unspeakably awful to have him take them back. Later—trying to figure out where things went wrong with Mickey—she thought it was the night he met Kate that his love began to sputter, to fizzle out.

"You're never going to be really with me, are you?" he said, staring her down. "You're always going to see yourself as bi. Your friends, they all make fun of straight people. I don't feel comfortable around them. They act like sex is just some kind of sport. That's not how you are, Shaz."

She sighed, a wavery, precrying kind of sigh. "They're not making fun of you, or us, or whatever, don't you see that? Don't you see how nice it was of Kate to come here tonight?"

But of course he wouldn't understand. You'd have to make him spend a year as a dyke; you'd have to put him inside a dark skin like hers; you'd have to estrange him from his family. How could Mickey be expected to understand? He belonged to a huge WASPy clan, relatives always inviting him to cocktail parties, his mother leaving messages on his machine like, "Your father told me that you got a job mixing for a trip-hop band. Congratulations, honey. I'm so proud of you."

Sometimes she felt sick with jealousy when she heard

messages like that. Shaz's mom was sweet, so sweet that you wanted to protect her from knowing about things like trip-hop and Pride marches and cakes with dicks on them. Whenever Shaz visited her mom, she pretended to be the Good Muslim Girl. She chatted with the cousins about med school; she wore cotton dresses and loafers; she told her mother that if all else failed, she would agree to an arranged marriage sometime in the far-distant future.

It exhausted her to be the Good Muslim Girl, and she could only keep the act going for a few days. That's why, when her mother had wanted to take Shaz and her brother to Karachi years ago, Shaz had refused. They went without her, sending letters that described the achingly white streets, women in pink and silver finery, minarets and mosques. That summer, living in Berkeley, Shaz had been exploring what turned out to be her own homeland: the drag bars in the Castro, the jubilant crowd of dykes at Pride Day, that sweet sweaty place inside a woman. The letters had piled up on her desk, and she hadn't known how to answer them.

How would Mickey ever understand what it was like to be a stranger to your own culture? How would he understand what it was like to be a stranger to just about everyone, to have a curve to your nose and a shade of skin that nobody could place? She was always getting asked "Where are you from? Where are you from?" Like it was any of their business.

Mickey would never understand any of this. And yet, that was part of the attraction. It made him exotic. He floated on a cloud of privilege, and once you were on that cloud with him, it was easy to forget the grime and stink of the city below.

Shaz hadn't minded Boston in the summer, the clammy heat and the greenish-gray bruise of pollution over the skyline, until she met Mickey. It used to be that when the city emptied out on the weekends, she'd think, "Good, they're gone." It had never occurred to her to wonder where all those people went. Now she knew. Her first June weekend with Mickey, he drove her up to his parents' house in Bar Harbor. They pulled into the driveway just after dark, stepping out of the car into the sudden silence of Maine. Or it seemed silent for a moment, until the noises swelled up around them—the throbbing of crickets, the smacking of waves against a shore somewhere just out of sight, the hiss of pine trees adjusting themselves in the wind. Shaz and Mickey followed a path of crumbling stones toward a strange crooked house with the date 1863 over its door. Inside it smelled of wood smoke; a decrepit golden retriever crept toward them, wagging its tail.

The next day, they flew through the water in a little boat, the sun dazzling on its sails. At sunset, they all gathered on the porch for drinks; Mickey's parents, his sister and brother-in-law, moved in slow motion, tangling their perfect tan legs over the arms of chairs. They squinted their eyes because of the sun, and discussed the neighbors in ironic, drawling voices.

"I just know she's going to put out that flag again," Mickey's mother said, and then turned to Shaz to explain.

"They've got an American flag so big you could wrap the house in it. They're real Mainers."

Shaz smiled, but she felt fake. It seemed like they'd been laughing at these neighbors, at these same old jokes, for years, and she would never be a part of it.

"You've been so quiet," Mickey said that night when they were in bed. "Are you okay?"

"Yeah, it's great here. I just don't know how to act around your family so I revert to my Good Muslim Girl personality."

She was thinking of herself at eight or nine, just before her parents split up, decked out for a visit from her grandmother in a poofy American dress and golden sandals. Her mother would have put on that blue-flowered *shalwar kameez* that always looked so psychedelic when it showed up later in snapshots. Her father would wear a crisp business suit, hair slicked back. The room would smell like *gulab jamuns,* a sickly sweetness cut with the almost chemical odor of rose water. And she would sit with her back perfectly straight in the little Bedouin chair. She pictured it like a snapshot, everyone stiff and formal and in their place.

After the divorce, they always seemed to be shut up in that dark, curtained house. Afterward, it was other people's living rooms; they were wafted into a world of cousins and friends. Anu who was studying to be a doctor. Vijaya who had married the Lebanese man. The Jindias, who were always en route to or just back from Karachi. Her mother would rattle away in Urdu, occasionally breaking into English to say, "What's wrong, Shazia? Why are you so cranky?"

Even then, Shaz was an outsider, the little girl in the corner who couldn't understand the language. So she got in the habit of tuning out, being in her own world. When she was about fourteen, she would lock herself in her room and put on a scratchy punk record and jerk herself off—a victim of that insatiable teenage horniness. She imagined what it would be like to be taken home by Iggy Pop or Patti Smith or Joe Strummer, naked with someone who understood her, whispering secrets.

One day, she discovered her brother's old guitar in the back of a closet. She began stroking its strings along to the records. When she got good enough to keep up with the melody line, Shaz could enter her own semi-erotic teenage fangirl bliss state. Playing along to "Because the Night," she would feel as if she were *touching* Patti Smith's voice, weaving herself inside and out of it.

Back then, before she'd ever had sex, she'd imagined love to be gooey, something you melted into. And then with her first boyfriend, Bobby, she learned that it was more a matter of friendship, more a matter of propping your feet up on someone's stomach while you watched late-night TV. Who knew that more than ten years later, when she least expected it, she'd find the fevered passion that actually lived up to her fourteen-year-old-girl masturbation fantasies?

Or at least that's how it had seemed in the beginning with Mickey. And then, even as things began to unravel, they had their moments—those mornings when they ate leftover scones from the bakery and drank lattes and then went back to bed for a long delirious fuck. The looks they'd shoot each other at parties or during band practice—a telepathy passing between them.

But more and more, the connection failed. "Sometimes I'm so in love with you and sometimes I'm not so sure," Mickey would say, and so she'd try even harder to twist herself into the woman he wanted.

She wore dresses. She cooked. She took care of the laundry, the clutter, the groceries. She told her friends, "I'm turning into my mother. And the scary thing is, I like it." She'd be standing there cutting up coriander, inhaling the sweet and soapy odor, when she'd suddenly flash on her mother. It hadn't been all bad between her parents—that's what she had just begun to understand. She remembered those nights when her father was expected for dinner; how her mother would take out the embroidered tablecloth, snap it in the air, and let it fall over the dining-room table. It was a magic trick to summon her father, who whisked into the house like one of the Islamic djins, huge and golden-skinned.

One day Shaz called her mother and said, "Amma, I've met a nice boy. He went to Harvard."

Her mother sighed, her breath uneven. "I'm so relieved, Shazia. What does he do?"

"Well," she said, suddenly wishing she'd never brought it up, "he's a musician. And the other thing, Amma? He's American."

"Oh, Shazia." Her mother sounded like she was going to

cry. Then she seemed to recover. "It's good you've met somebody, though. That's a start. I worry about you all the time. All the time."

"I know." Over the phone line, she'd felt close to her mother again. They used to be so close when they waited together for her father to come home—they longed for him the way you crave lightning on a humid summer afternoon. He'd yell at you for leaving toys in the driveway, or he'd gather you up in his arms and kiss your ears; either way, at least it was a change from the drowsy darkness of the ordinary.

And now, after Shaz said good-bye to her mother and hung up the phone, she indulged herself. For just a moment, she imagined what it would be like if she married Mickey. "You know I had other hopes for you," her mother would say, meaning a Pakistani doctor. "But now at least I don't have to worry. My mind is at ease." She could imagine her mother beaming up at her, one hand around her waist.

Shaz stopped herself there. After all, there was no reason to believe she'd ever get married—even if she could make herself want to. She and Mickey had so many bad spells now—hysterical fights, days when he wanted to be alone, times when they slept with as much space between them as possible.

One morning he was silent through breakfast, and then skulked off to his studio, not even thanking her for the eggs she'd made. She had tried to be cool about it, padding around the kitchen, cleaning up. But finally she just couldn't stand the silence anymore. She walked over to him, put her hands on his neck. It practically killed her, the way he flinched from her touch.

"What did I do wrong?" she said. "I don't even know why you're mad."

He had nudged her hands off his neck and stood up. "You didn't do anything wrong. That's just the problem." He breathed out a sigh. "I hate how I'm acting."

"Well then stop it."

"I've tried." He raked his hands through his hair. "It's not your fault. It's me."

She felt her face get hot. "What do you mean?" she said. "If there's a problem, it's ours."

"No," he said angrily—though he wasn't angry at her, she knew that. "We've tried and it doesn't work."

"Look," she said, "it's been hard for us both, with the tour coming up and everything. We're both worried." She hated the pleading sound in her own voice, the way she was trying to paste a kind of normalness over this conversation.

"I'll tell you the truth," he said in a quiet voice that was somehow dead. "I'm wondering how to do it. How to break up." He seemed to be talking not to her, but to someone who stood just behind her.

For a moment she thought her knees would go out. But in fact she had stood taller and spit out, "That's it? That's what you've been thinking about this whole time? That you're just going to give up on me?"

"Yes," he said in a small voice.

"Look at me when you say that," she said. "The least you can do is look at me." They had already broken up—she knew that. In an instant, she'd gone from being Mickey's girlfriend to being something else. She could sense her own anger and grief hovering around her like bats, waiting to descend. But right now she was curious. She wanted to find out what this new woman—herself, her single self— would do.

"I know this is going to be hard for you. But we'll get through it," he said.

Shaz narrowed her eyes. "What are you talking about?"

"I've known I should do this for a while, but I put it off because I didn't want—"

"What? To hurt me? Please."

"I really don't want to lose you." His voice wavered. He was still looking at the ground. "I don't want to lose you as a friend—or as a bass player." Suddenly she realized he was actually scared of her. That's what blew Shaz away. How long had he been scared of her?

"As a bass player?" she heard herself bark. And then she watched this new woman snatch up her stuff and hurry out, past the place where the sun quivered on the floor in the morning, past the practice space, past the three mailboxes, past the black El Camino parked in front of his building. She just kept on going, along the river, clasping her coat around herself because of the wind that cut across the gray water. The old sense of being alone welled up in her in a way it hadn't for more than a year. It was unbearable.

She went home and took a long shower. Then she lay in bed in her long-disused room and listened to her favorite albums—still Patti Smith, but also Liz Phair and Big

Mama Thornton. In Mickey's apartment, they'd listened to jazz. Now, after such a long absence, these songs seemed like neglected but faithful friends, soothing her, reminding her who she'd been before Mickey. That night, she eased back into aloneness like someone wading into the Maine ocean, inching forward into the freezing cold water, until it felt good. The next day, he left a message on her machine: He hoped she was doing okay. He wanted to talk. Would she come to practice? She played his voice over a few times. Some sensible side of herself had taken over, and she knew better than to call him. It was her self-sufficient core— what he used to call her invulnerability—that she listened to now.

"Tell him I'm not here," she instructed her roommates. He left panicky messages. Where was she? The CD would be out soon. Hadn't she agreed to go on tour? Hadn't she signed a contract? Weren't they all depending on her? A week later, she found the CD shoved through her mail slot. The five of them stared out from the cover. Mickey was in the middle, glowering. And Shaz stood next to him—or rather, the old Shaz, the woman who peered from behind his arm, wearing a cocktail dress and lipstick. The day they posed for that, she remembered, Mickey had convinced her to bring the dress along to the photographer's studio. She'd put it on, feeling like she was in drag, in drag as a woman.

She walked back into the house and threw the CD on the couch. The house hung around her, silent and expectant. And she stood in the middle of it, waiting to see what would happen.

This is what happened: She worked her butt off and became manager of the Eat Me store in Cambridge. She joined the Exes in her nonexistent spare time. She fooled around with a bunch of people and eventually found a new lover; she and Valerie had a friendly, three-nights-a-week relationship that let them both work a lot. And then, just recently she'd moved into her own apartment. She'd never had her own place before, and it made her happier than maybe anything else ever had. Sitting at the little table she'd nailed together herself, she'd be overcome by a sense of possibility. She could do anything here.

That was part of the reason she hated the idea of touring with the Exes. She'd finally escaped the dirty dishes, the grungy living rooms of group houses, and the roommates knocking on her door. And now, just when she had her own space, the Exes wanted her to cram into the van with them for six weeks. Ever since yesterday—ever since she'd had that fight with Hank—she'd entertained a dizzying new idea. She could quit the band. In her newly free evenings, she would read and listen to music, make furniture, maybe even write her own songs.

She'd try it out tonight anyway; she'd decided to blow off practice so she could just hang out, listening to music and patching her favorite pair of pants. She was just about to sit down and get out her sewing kit, to sink into that deep solitude she craved, when the door began rattling.

When she peered through the peephole, there was a fisheye version of Lilly, with a big nose inside a tiny head.

"How'd you get in the building?" Shaz said, opening the door.

"Oh, I just followed someone in." Lilly was wearing little-girl barrettes, a polyester dress, glittery slippers, and a wool coat. She looked like she'd thrown on the coat and run down the street. Lilly and Dieter lived only a few blocks away. "I knew you'd be home," Lilly said. "I saw you on your bike, going past."

"Look," Shaz said, "don't bother. I know you guys are all mad at me. I don't want to talk about it, okay?"

Lilly walked into the apartment and dumped her coat on the ground. "Calm down. I'm on your side, Shaz. I know Hank is being a total jerk. That's why I'm here."

They sat near the stove. Without asking, Lilly put on water to boil. "Where's your tea?" Lilly opened and closed the cabinets. "Oh, here." She's set two mugs, honey and milk on the table. "You know, it's strange," she said, "I've never seen your apartment before. You keep it so neat. And all the shelves and stuff. It's like a ship."

"Yeah. It's so small; no one comes over really except Val," Shaz said.

Lilly stalked around, picking things up and examining them. She seemed bewitched by all the cubbyholes and compartments. Suddenly, Shaz saw her own apartment through Lilly's eyes: the futon rolled up in the corner with a silk *dupatta* thrown on top; the shelves and shelves of LPs; the wooden trays full of hand-labeled spices; the acoustic guitar and the electric bass, both on their stands. The place suddenly glowed with mystery, every object glittering like a tool for some secret task.

Lilly touched the tiny glass jars full of tinctures. "How do you keep this place so neat? Do you actually live here, or are you usually at Val's?"

"No, I'm here," Shaz said, pouring some honey into her tea. "It's running a store. At work I have to keep track of about three hundred different cake decorations. It warps your mind. You start organizing everything."

Lilly sat down. In the closet-sized kitchen, they were so close that their knees almost touched. "Listen, I know how you feel about this whole tour thing." Lilly looked down into her tea, stirring it. She glanced up again, catching Shaz with those gold eyes. "I mean, Hank's done his number on me a million times. It really sucks when he starts acting like you're his slave."

"What did he tell you about me?" Shaz cautiously took a sip of her tea. She wasn't a tea drinker usually, and it calmed her to have this steaming cup in her hands.

"Oh, the usual. He said you were ungrateful and you were sabotaging us. I was like, 'Hank, give me a break. Shazia has a fucking life. You can't *command* her to just take off for six weeks.'"

Shaz looked out the window, at the shingles of the building next door. For some reason she was embarrassed. "Thanks," she said.

"It would suck if you didn't go on tour with us. Really suck. But we can deal. I mean, this isn't Maoist China. This is a free country, right? A friggin' capitalist country, and we've got all that money from Bronco. We can always pay someone to go with us."

"Maybe Chet," Shaz said. Her own voice sounded far away, like someone else's.

"Oh God. Wouldn't Chet love that. He'd pee in his pants." She sipped her tea. "What a depressing thought, though—having him instead of you. I'd really miss you."

Shaz rested her head on her hands. "It's so hard. I mean, I hate the idea of someone playing my bass lines, you know? But I have to get out now, before this thing gets too crazy."

"Maybe you could play with us when we're in town, and then we could use Chet or somebody whenever we tour," Lilly said. "Would that be okay?"

"I guess. Maybe. Anyway, this is making me sad. Let's talk about something else." Shaz got up to put on a tape.

"Okay, but I just want to tell you something. It doesn't have to do with you that much, or the tour, but I just . . . I think you should know about it." Lilly's voice cracked and then trailed off. Shaz had never seen her look so serious. "Remember when that gossip came out in *The Sound* about me and Hank?" she said.

"Yeah. That was just someone slagging you, I thought. You just laughed it off."

"I was pretending to laugh it off. Actually, I was shitting in my pants. It was true, all of it. Hank and I were fooling around." Lilly licked her lips.

"You're kidding." Shaz's hand froze on the tape deck; she'd suddenly forgotten which button to push.

"It just about ruined my life. Of course Dieter saw it, and

I had to tell him what had been going on. You never knew about any of this?"

"No," Shaz said. It was always a revelation to her, the mess that other people made of their lives. She didn't understand how it was so easy for so many people to lie to their lovers, to let secrets grow like subterranean mosses. "I can't believe I never noticed. But now that I think back, it's obvious. Things were really tense for a while."

"No shit," Lilly said. "I've been through hell. Dieter went nuts and destroyed a lot of my artwork."

"When was this?"

"I don't know. Maybe two months ago."

"So is it okay now?"

"Yeah." Lilly was oddly calm, taking a sip of her tea. She seemed so different than the usual Lilly, that hyperactive girlie-girl who jabbered away. She had some new stillness about her, a certain poise. When had she become this other person? How had Shaz missed this transformation?

"It must have been awful," Shaz said. "I'm sorry I didn't help you out or anything. Why didn't you tell me?"

"For the good of the band, Hank and I decided to not make a big deal about it. He and I stopped hanging out, though we still get along okay." Lilly put her head on her hands.

Shaz leaned against the wall, not knowing what to say. "Well, I wish I'd helped you."

"Nobody could have done anything," Lilly said. "Jesus, it was so awful. I thought I'd lost Dieter, and that's when I realized how much I loved him. I couldn't believe how stupid I'd been.

"But the weird thing was, cheating on him turned out to be the best thing I'd ever done. There were real problems between us, and things had to get worse before they could get better, you know? We were both so scared to lose each other. We talked it out and had this amazing breakthrough where we realized we were really committed and stuff. That's when we decided, um . . ." Lilly looked down, fell silent.

The apartment seemed even smaller now. It was as if they were pressed up against each other, breathing together. "What?" Shaz said.

"Well, to have a baby."

Shaz felt the blood drain out of her lips. "Are you sure that's a good idea?"

"I'm already pregnant." Lilly laughed, her old self. "I just found out. See? This is herb tea. I'm off caffeine and ciga-rettes, didn't you notice?"

"No. I feel like an idiot that I didn't pick any of this up. I mean, you said you were quitting a few weeks ago, but I didn't think about it too much."

Lilly waved her hand. "Oh, don't worry. Only the other smokers noticed. They've all been watching me with eagle eyes, waiting for me to slip up. That's how they figured out I was preggers at work. I had to, like, have a damn good rea-son for quitting or else everyone would be mad at me."

"So what about the tour? Are you going?"

"Oh yeah, of course. I'm in total promotion overdrive. I've been sending flirty letters to every college-station dee-jay in America. I'm so psyched. But Hank—"

"Oh yeah, I hadn't thought of that," Shaz said. "Have you told him?"

"Are you kidding? Why do you think he freaked when you backed out of the tour? His lead singer is knocked up and a few days later his bassist decides she won't travel. It's, like, attack of the rebellious women. At this point, he's probably cowering in his room, waiting for Gloria Steinem to come and cut off his balls."

Despite herself, Shaz burst out laughing. She shook her head and rubbed her cheeks, but she couldn't stop. Really, it was awful that Lilly was pregnant—she seemed to be having a kid just to make up with Dieter. But Shaz loved it, too, the impulsiveness of it. "So you're going to be on tour, puking in the motel rooms and eating pickles or whatever. And Hank's going to be trying to keep you under control."

Lilly snorted tea out of her nose, and then doubled over with giggles. "Yeah, I really got him this time, didn't I? How's he going to manage this one?"

"Oh, Lilly, maybe I'll go," Shaz said, still trying to stop laughing. "Just to see it."

Lilly jumped up and hugged her then. "Oh, please, pretty please with a cherry on top. Please come. I'll just die if you don't."

Shaz pulled away. "No, I shouldn't have said that. I'll miss you, but this is the last thing I need. I'm just getting my life together. You understand that, don't you?"

"Yeah, it's okay," Lilly said mournfully. "But it's not going to be the same with Chet. He thinks he's such a bass stud. It's so much fun when you rock out with me."

Something between them had loosened, some wall between them had dropped. "I really have to think about it. I need some time," Shaz said.

"Listen, you don't have to tell me," Lilly said. "But I wish I knew what messed you up so much—like, why you feel so out of control and stuff. In all this time, you've never really told me."

Shaz stared down at the table, the worn grain of the wood. She ran her fingernail through the soft part, making a mark. "You don't really want to know, do you? Do you really care?"

Lilly rolled her eyes. "Duh. I care."

"It's just that I'm ashamed of how ugly it got when I was in Sluggo," Shaz said. Then she found herself spilling out the story; she'd never told the whole thing to anyone, even Val. Just pieces. She had only told pieces of it before—maybe because it had never seemed like a story in her head. Trying to remember, she could only glimpse bits of it that didn't go together. Who was she back then? Not the Shaz of the apartment with all its pigeonholes and nooks and rows of bottles, as self-contained as the cabin of a ship.

Now, when she tried to explain it to Lilly, her voice kept faltering. She kept having to say, "No, wait, I forgot to explain something." She wanted Lilly to understand how she was not herself for a year and then—bursting out of Mickey's loft and striding along the river—she was again.

"After we broke up, I knew I just had to get away," she said. "Put it all behind me and move on, you know? It had all been a big mistake and I didn't want to make any more mistakes. So I stayed away from him. Obviously, that meant I couldn't be in his band anymore. The upshot was, I dropped out two weeks before they were supposed to go on tour."

"Oh shit," Lilly said appreciatively. "He must have freaked."

"No kidding. The asshole actually threatened to sue me. I guess I'd signed a contract. There was this one day when I came home and I had a message from a lawyer on my machine. It was just some stupid friend of Mickey's, but I lost it. I think I cried for hours. I could just picture myself forced to go on tour, in all those foreign countries, having to take Mickey's orders. Then, luckily, my roommate Tracy came home and listened to the message and she just cracked up. She thought it was the funniest thing she'd ever heard. I never called him back. I didn't pick up the phone until they were out of town."

Lilly shook her head, chuckling. "Excellent. Too bad they're doing so well now."

"Yeah, I know. Did you see the thing in *Details,* with them modeling vintage clothes?"

Lilly leaned forward, her eyes narrowed. "Go with us. We're going to kick ass. We're going to be famous. That would be the ultimate revenge on that asshole. I swear, we're right on the cusp. What if Bronco picks us as their Artists of the Year over Sluggo? Wouldn't that kill him?"

Shaz laughed. "Come on, that's a stupid reason for me to go—just to get revenge on some guy."

And she realized as she said this that it was true. Even six months ago, the revenge fantasies were still bubbling up in her mind. Sometimes she imagined Mickey coming to an Exes show; he'd see what a good player she'd become without him—for she had. Sometimes she imagined what it would be like if they ran into each other on the street; she'd be holding hands with Val, of course, and nod a dismissive hello to him. But now, she just couldn't be bothered to hate him anymore.

"I let the Mickey thing eat away at me for a while," she said. "But I'm over it now."

"Well, I can see why you don't want to go on this tour. I mean, after all that, you're probably not so psyched to let another rock Nazi run your life." Lilly leaned forward. Her eyes looked as flat and strange as cats' eyes. "Hank's not as bad as that guy you used to go out with, but he has his moments. And I'll tell you something: He gets all weird around you. He's really nice to me, but he acts like a jerk to you."

As soon as Lilly said it, Shaz recognized it as true. Hank wanted her the way Mickey had wanted her. He wanted to be the one who discovered her, to claim her, to name her, to show her off to the world. He longed to rip the talent out of her and take it for his own. "You're right," Shaz said in a shaky voice. "It's not me. It's him."

"God," Lilly rolled her eyes. "Of course it's him. What did you think? You think it's your fault?" She reached into her bag like she was fumbling for cigarettes, then stopped herself. "Yeah, well anyway, don't let it get you down." She flipped her wrist to look at her watch. "I'll tell them you're not coming to practice tonight. If he freaks out, I'll deal with him, okay? It's not your problem anymore."

So that's how they left it. Supposedly, Shaz had what she wanted. But later, standing by the sink to do the dishes, something about it nagged at her. She kept remembering that summer after freshman year—the summer that Amma and Gopal went to Karachi and she stayed in Berkeley. She'd had a mailbox in the lobby of her building that she opened with a little golden key. Usually all the mail was for her roommates. But once in a while she'd find a letter inside in her mother's neat writing. "We're preparing for a wedding today, one of your grandmother's neighbors," the letter might read, and suddenly Shaz could imagine it all: the smell of the cooking and the voices mumbling in Urdu, that close childhood whirl of people, the touch of their hands.

Shaz had been so lonely that summer. How could she have forgotten that? She had loved biking around to the bars, flirting with girls, but other times the anonymity of it scared her. There was nobody in the city who really knew her. Sometimes she'd walk down the street, gazing into strangers' faces and thinking, "I could pretend to be anybody and they'd believe me." Then a horrible blahness would descend over her. She'd stop in the middle of the sidewalk; wherever she'd been heading to would seem like a stupid place. Why go? Why do anything?

And here it was again, the feeling she remembered from that summer. She stopped washing the dishes and let her hands float in the soapy water.

Across the river, she knew, the three of them were gathered in that basement room, where it smelled of musty clothes and damp cement. She could picture Lilly curled up on top of her amp, and Walt perched on his tiny stool, and Hank pacing back and forth. They would be talking about what to do without Shaz, how to replace her.

Under her hands, the dishes moved like heavy fish, drifting away from her touch. The night was her own. She could do whatever she wanted. Was this freedom? She hadn't been prepared for it to feel so blah. She hadn't known how scary it was.

Walt

Walt is half out of it from last night, a sold-out show in Ann Arbor and then troubled sleep on the moldy shag rug in the house belonging to some friend of a friend. After five hours of sleep, they peeled themselves off the floor. Walt has been driving ever since then. Only one fight so far this morning. Lilly threw a tantrum because she wanted to stop in Battle Creek, home of the breakfast cereal. After three weeks on the road, Walt can't even remember the last time he ate breakfast cereal. It's been coffee, cigarettes, Zoloft, flat beer, Twizzlers, diner food.

Now it's late morning, and he and Hank are sitting in the van, waiting for the women to pee. Fucking cold outside. The gas station attendant runs out to take people's money and then runs back into his little booth. The van is not exactly a tropical paradise either. Hank, in the passenger seat, has on his knit Fudgsicle cap and is clutching a blanket. Walt notices how burned-out Hank looks—stubble on his chin and bags under his eyes—and thinks he must look just as bad or worse. He can smell his own stale sweat, wafting out of the neck hole of his sweater—a thick wool one that reeks of wet dog.

"Hey," Hank is asking him, "what was that with Gina? You know, up until now, I wasn't even sure you liked girls. But last night, geez . . . The way you moved in on her was legendary."

"I really like her," Walt hears his own voice crack. He glances nervously toward the gas station bathroom.

"I don't think they saw you." Hank sips his coffee. "They were out guarding the van or something. So come on, man, spill."

"I don't know, it just kind of happened." Walt's embarrassed, but also honored to be bonding, to have Hank talk to him in that way he does with his friends from work. Walt has hung out with those guys after shows a bunch of times. There's a crude kind of intimacy among them. They delve into all the matters that they wouldn't dare discuss if their girlfriends were around: the *Penthouse*s in the stockroom at work with sticky pages; the weirder kinks of their lust; the difficulties of seducing a woman when you know your underwear is baggy and stained.

Those guys glance at Walt conspiratorially while they talk. But they never turn to him and say, "So what about you? What's up with your sex life?" Maybe it's obvious that he has nothing worth telling. Every time he's with those guys, Walt wishes he had something juicy to confess, some coin in the economy of sexual secrets. The only woman he's slept with in the last year is a chemistry fellow who worked down the hall from him for a while. Her button-down shirts, her pale eyes swimming behind glasses, her obsession with learning the Klingon language—she was not a woman he could present to those guys as a sexual conquest.

But now, this morning in the van, he finally has something to tell. His own voice sounds strange as he tries to linger over the details the way Hank's friends would. "I already knew Gina from around Boston," he says. "We'd hung out at parties. It always seemed like we hit it off, but it never occurred to me to, um . . . I don't know. Last night we were kind of drunk, and we were leaning over to hug each other good-bye, and then suddenly we were making out for like ten minutes."

Hank drum-rolls his hands on the dashboard of the van. "Woooooo. Excellent. You know, you're the only one who can legally get any action in this band." He means that everyone else has a girlfriend or boyfriend. "You're really, really lucky. I'm going to have to live vicariously through you."

Walt furrows his brow. "You think *I'm* lucky? Anita's so great and you guys are in love and everything."

"Yeah, I hear you. It does suck being single. But on tour it's different. You're up on stage looking out at them, and you know that if you want to get laid it's all out there for the taking. All you want, man. And you'll be out of town the next day."

Walt squirms. "Yeah," he says, "I don't like to admit it, but I've had thoughts like that."

"So, but tell me, what was the upshot with Gina? Did you guys make plans or something?"

Walt starts to answer, but then Hank waves his hand. "Wait, sssh. The girls."

For some reason, this makes Walt crack up. Suddenly, he and Hank are both laughing hysterically.

"What's wrong with you guys?" Shaz says, climbing into the back of the van.

"Come on," Lilly says, dragging in behind her. "Don't laugh at me. I'm feeling really sick."

Walt pulls the van out onto the highway, and they all settle into driving mode, saying little to each other because it's too hard to shout over the whine of the engine.

They're whizzing over a flat highway, past the frozen tundra of Michigan, the monotony broken only now and then by a green sign that tempts you to exit to some mysterious Midwestern city. Jackson. Lansing. Kalamazoo. And he's thinking about last night, that moment when he was drumming to the song "Gore," waving his hair around letting the sweat fly off his face, that moment when he actually felt like a real rock star.

They had been playing to maybe two hundred people—which was some kind of record for them. True, most of the crowd showed up to see the headlining band. But there was this contingent of peroxided college-student babes with pierced nostrils who bobbed up front—their own fans.

The Exes were having their fifteen minutes. That's how Lilly would have put it. Usually they play to half-empty clubs or frat-boy audiences that ignore them. And then once or twice they stumble into some town and discover they have *groupies* and the club is packed. Which means some college-station deejay must have been playing their CD and the locals are under the impression that the Exes are a famous indie band like Boss Hog or the Royal Trux. "It's our fifteen minutes, y'all," Lilly will say, to remind them that they better enjoy it while it lasts.

Last night was the most intense burst of fame so far. Weird fame, because the audience only wanted to hear one song, "Gore." Some deejay must have really liked that track, played it over and over on the college station. Every time they finished a song, the groupie contingent would start chanting, "'Gore,' 'Gore,' 'Gore'" like nothing else counted.

Lilly turned it into a joke. "Uh, I want to introduce you to the band," she'd said, half swallowing the mike. Loud cheers. "We're the All-Gore Band. And my name is Lesley Gore." Then she did a quick solo on her guitar, went into a few bars of the song "It's My Party."

"This here," Lilly said, gesturing at Shaz, "is Tipper Gore." And weirdly, Shaz—who didn't like anything new thrown at her—rose to the occasion. She played this heavy funk bass line and growled into her mike, "Yeah, and anyone who's using explicit language out there—I'm going to slap you around."

"And this," Lilly had said, without missing a beat, "is Al Gore." Hank had stepped forward, guitar strapped around his body, and put a toy-store melodica to his lips to squawk out a few notes.

That was when Walt started to sense it out there, the audience's pent-up energy, how they all wanted to explode. There was a feeling you got when you *had* the audience. Like they were a kind of orchestra. Like you were conducting them.

"And this guy back here," Lilly said, waving her hand at Walt. "This guy is, um, um . . ." And there was the dreadful moment when she seemed to have blanked out. But then, right on cue, someone from the crowd yelled, "Gore Vidal."

"Yeah, Gore Vidal, whoever that is," Lilly had said. And Walt *knew* what to do next. It was the kind of knowing you have in your body. He lifted up one drumstick, held it there a minute to tease the crowd, then crashed the stick onto the high hat and launched into the weird syncopated solo that was the beginning of "Gore." Shaz was right there. She came in on the eighth beat. Then they were all there, the grinding of Hank and Lilly's guitars, and Lilly's voice screaming, "They found me in the dumpster cut in two. That's the last time I go on a date with you. I'm not your porn, I'm not your gore, I'm one pissed-off pussy and I'm coming after you." She was bending over, curling into the mike, flailing one arm around. And the audience pushed close. It was scary almost. Like they wanted to eat you.

Sometimes when all the factors are right you suddenly click in. You're *there*. You aren't playing the music anymore—it's going through you, like electricity. After all, the body is a drum set: the heart is a high hat; the lungs, a bass drum; the blood, a pulsing snare. You could kill a person by hitting him with enough sound at just the right frequency—a vibration that would set the lungs or heart or liver singing. And sometimes you want that. You want to find the one perfect note that will shatter everything.

That's how he'd always thought of it. The impulse to self-destruct. But now he realizes Hank is right too. It's sex that electrifies you. All those women bobbing up front, swarming close, lapping you with their eyes. Enough of that groupie adoration and your mind gets warped.

Years ago, he read a cheesy rock bio of Led Zeppelin. There was one night when Robert Plant and Jimmy Page and the others had all been holed up in their hotel room, bored and coked up. For some reason, they had a shark in there with them. And they convinced one of the groupies to have sex with a shark, to stick its body up inside her.

He'd wondered about that. Why, if you were famous and filthy rich, would you bother to stoop to such a junior-high-school kind of prank? But now he's beginning to understand. There's something inherently juvenile about being in a band. He keeps flashing on the time in eighth grade when Linda Rubens told him she didn't want her locker next to his because he stank. And now he likes to imagine what would happen if he were transported back to Woodrow Wilson Junior High—this time with his long hair and his drumsticks. Linda Rubens would be down on her knees, begging forgiveness, begging for the locker next to his.

* * *

Last night he'd come off the stage with trembling legs, totally wiped out. People had been swarming around him. He suddenly had a beer in his hand. Then Gina appeared beside him. "That was great," she said. Gina was the bass player for the Brood, the band that was going on after them.

Walt tried to stammer an answer.

"I know," Gina laughed. "You're fried. It's okay,"

And later—after she got off the stage—they'd hung out in a corner together, pressed close. When he had to leave, she'd yelled into his ear, "I'll see you in Chicago."

Maybe Walt was still buzzed from the show, still feeling like a rock god. Usually when he wanted to kiss a woman, he messed it up—he hesitated, waiting for just the right angle and pause in conversation where it would seem natural, and by the time he was ready she would have moved away. But last night, he knew just when to bend over her small, still-sweaty face. He'd locked eyes with her, and then just sort of fallen onto her lips. She tasted like cherry Kool-Aid. As they twisted tongues, she pushed something into his mouth, a slick flat lozenge. A cough drop. He passed it back through his lips and felt her tongue take it. She broke away, wiped her face against his shirt.

"I always thought you were cute," she said. "But you never seemed to like me."

And then Hank was calling him. He had to go. But he'd see her soon: they were opening for the Brood in Chicago and then in Minneapolis and L.A.

Getting to open for the Brood was the Exes' big break.

The Brood was famous, at least in indie-rock kind of way. Their video had played on MTV once—at three in the morning. He'd seen an article about them in *Spin;* there'd been a lime-yellow, wide-angle photo that made it look like the four of them had just stepped out of some psychedelic netherworld, dripping in acid colors.

And now, Gina Jeffers—the pouty butch one, the one who rode her skateboard in that rock video, the one who wrote a song that sends shivers down his back—Gina wanted him.

It's almost two o'clock now. Walt slumps in the back seat of the van, huddled inside his coat. His feet are freezing and he's stuffed toilet paper in his ears to try to tune out the shrieking hum of the engine. The van smells like rancid peanut butter, sweat, machine oil, and rotten bananas.

He has that trapped, stuck-in-time feeling. It reminds him of when he was stuck in the loony bin—the ward with a puke yellow rug turning gray in places from all the cigarette ash. That's what people did in there—smoke. Smoke and watch game shows, while the windows blazed with daylight. He'd lie on the floor, plug up his ears, and read, trying to tune out the craziness around him. At least in the loony bin the seats didn't vibrate.

It's impossible to read in the van: it rattles so badly that the letters on the page buzz around like fruit flies. All he can do is lie here, trying not to roll off his seat when they hit a bump. That's the worst part about being on tour—you can't work on any of your own projects. Instead, you just have to wait around, zone out, guard the equipment, ride in the van. He can't remember the last time he's spent so many hours a day spacing out. He's been in school practically his whole life, always had a research paper hanging over his head, a pile of books crammed into his bag to read in spare moments waiting for the bus. Every moment packed with constructive activity.

Before he left Boston, he promised his advisor that he would isolate one of the smell receptors in the human nose, take a sample, grow crystals from the protein, and then write up a paper for the journals. Walt is supposed to be finished a month from now. There's no way he will be. Those stupid protein crystals take forever to grow. He managed to get some started before he left, but they've probably croaked by now. He gets anxious just thinking about those petri dishes stowed in the lab back at Harvard, his name scrawled across the plastic lids, the dead cells inside.

When everyone else is watching reruns on the cable TV in their motel room, Walt finds his mind wandering back to those petri dishes. In his imagination, he's untwisting the DNA, running a finger over its pieces, testing each one like a piano key, trying to figure out how the signals flow.

"Walt, what are you doing? You're staring into space again," they tease him. They don't know where he is. They don't know that he's whirling around inside his own blood, or delicately exploring a corn gene, or encouraging an epithelial cell to divide.

When he was a kid, he thought this was normal. He assumed that everyone lived inside the massive dome of his or her own thoughts, a snail shell you could curl into at any time. His parents had been like that, anyway. Once he saw his father kneeling in the garden, digging furiously in the soil while he muttered to himself, growls and barks of gibberish. It turned out his dad was listening to a tape, trying to learn Russian while he weeded.

No wonder Walt ended up being such an obsessive kid. He'd spend hours in the basement building his models or taking apart old machines. Even when he had to pee he couldn't tear himself away from his projects to go upstairs to the bathroom. Instead, he'd dull the pain in his bladder by shoving his dick between his legs. And then he grew up and went to grad school. Basically, it was the adult version of being in the basement with his dick stuck between his legs. He'd stay at the lab until three in the morning and then go home and sit hunched over his keyboard or the tape recorder, trying to put together some piece of music. He lived in a trance, ignoring the pinch of his body's pains and his own loneliness.

Or at least, that's how it had been up until two years ago when he had his breakdown. The shrink had called it a major depressive episode, but Walt preferred the word "breakdown." His life was a faulty system that had stopped working. One day he started trembling, every touch on his skin like sandpaper. So he checked into the bin for a while, got himself dosed up, and then tried to figure out how to redesign the system, his life.

By the time he got out, Walt knew exactly what to do. He had come up with an elegant theory. If he wanted to be happy, he had to learn how to be a normal person. So first thing, he quit grad school. Then he looked for the right clothes. He bought his new outfit, what he thought of as his "normal suit," at a department store—a white cotton sweater and khaki pants. After that, he went down and got himself a job at the post office. By the time he was ready to start work, the white sweater was covered with stains, so he was glad to get his uniform—those crisp pants with the stripe running up each side, the button-down shirt with the insignia on it, and, best of all, the pith helmet. None of his coworkers at the Central Square branch had opted to wear the pith helmet, which Walt couldn't understand. It was the pith helmet that had made him want to be a mail carrier in the first place. It signified that you were on a safari through the yards and front hallways of Cambridge, an adventure in the wilderness of ordinary life.

At least, for the first month or so it seemed like an adventure. But after his initial love affair with normalcy, he realized he just wasn't cut out for it. His coworkers were nice, but he just couldn't figure out how to fit in with them. They talked about barhopping and TV stars, diets and cars. He tried to join their conversation, but he always seemed to say the wrong thing. He wanted to act like a regular guy, and instead he sounded like Noam Chomsky. He'd intend to make some simple remark about Oprah, and then find himself lecturing his coworkers about Oprah and imperialism. And so Phase One of the Walt Normalcy Project came to an abrupt halt.

* * *

It's almost dark when they pull up in front of the brick townhouse where they're staying in Wicker Park. Kelly opens the door, smiling, dark hair pulled up on her head and pierced with a chopstick.

"Hey, you guys," she says, and hugs Hank. She's an old girlfriend of his. Her place is huge with painted white brick walls, like a movie version of an artist's apartment. "My friends are so jealous that I'm having a band stay here," she says. "And then I came home today, and I had a message from the Brood's tour manager on my machine. That made me feel so cool." Kelly keeps up this stream of chatter while she bustles around offering them beers and food.

Walt drinks half a beer—with the Zoloft it hardly takes anything to get him tipsy now—and sinks into the hot pink chair Kelly made in art school. He's fried to the point where it feels good just to sit here on solid land, to suck down the brown rice she's handed out.

"Hey, Kelly," Hank says, "if you really want to be cool, why don't you come with us and meet the Brood? I was thinking we could swing by their hotel." And then—does Walt imagine this?—Hank winks at him.

A few minutes later, Hank's on the cordless. "Yeah, we're pretty toasted too, but we were thinking of checking out this cocktail bar."

When they're about to leave, Shaz says, "I don't have the energy. If it's okay with you, Kelly, I just want to hang out here and make some calls." Shaz hates group activities; whenever they have some free time, she asks to be dropped off places—a thrift store she spotted out the window of the van or a café where she can write letters. In the old days, Walt might have tagged along with her. He used to feel so awkward around Lilly and Hank that he would cling to Shaz. Or maybe he was wary of Lilly and Hank because of that crowd they belonged to, the ones who got drunk at the Middle East every night. Shaz called those people rock snots. The women sat in clusters, everything on them protruding like quills—black fingernails and cigarettes and fake eyelashes and high heels.

Eventually, Walt realized Hank and Lilly were different from those club people, and in the past few months he's become pretty close to them. He calls Hank when he's depressed; and Lilly, she seems able to sense it. She'll ruffle his hair and say, "Waltie, why are you sad? Don't you want to drum on the walls today?" He feels pretty comfortable around them, but lately it seems like he has nothing to say to Shaz. Strange how he'd drifted so far away from her.

Now he glances across the room, trying to figure out whether she's pissed off or not. She's washing down her vitamin pills with the herbal tea in her thermos. She's hunched over the table, still wearing her man's wool coat. Her expression is pinched and inward.

And suddenly he sees her for the first time without the erotic glow that's always seemed to surround her. She looks like an old woman. Not her face—for her lips still have that pout to them, her eyebrows are dark slashes that make her look Spanish. It's the way she sits; she moves around gingerly, as if she's shy of touching the table, the plate, the glass. When did she turn into this fragile and spinsterish person? He remembers when he met her at a party in San Francisco—what was it?—four years ago. She'd been curled on the couch, watching everything through narrowed eyes. He'd thought then that she was so self-possessed, the way she didn't care if anyone saw her sitting by herself. But now he wonders, has she always been like this?

He feels guilty leaving her that night. He senses that Shaz would rather he stayed, that she misses him. "See you later," he says, trying to catch her eye, but she's already heading for the phone.

And then they're in Kelly's vintage Impala, careening through the streets of Chicago with the New York Dolls blasting from the tape player. She pulls into the parking garage of some big hotel and soon they're walking down a plush, silent hall looking for room 503.

David the drummer opens the door. "Want anything from the minibar?" he asks.

After that, time speeds up. The room fills with people: Hank and Lilly and Kelly and Walt and David and Gina and Phoebe the singer and Mimi the lead guitarist. Next thing, everyone is down in the garage, piling into Kelly's car, smooshing into each other on the bench seats. Gina crawls in over the bodies and sits across his and David's laps.

They end up at some bar with furniture that looks like it came from a funeral home. They're crammed around a table, ordering Rob Roys and Tom Collinses and Manhattans, all those ironic drinks.

Everyone seems to be trying to push Gina and him to-gether. "Here," David says, "you slide in here," and he makes sure Gina's in the booth beside Walt.

Usually, Walt needs this kind of help. He's a failure at flirting. Or rather, he's always regarded flirting as a moral failure—it's too fake. When he has a crush on a woman, he tries to take the high ground and be sincere. "We should get together. We should hang out and talk," he might say to her. But there's something wrong with this method. He always seems to creep women out.

Or most women. Gina is different, the way Shaz had been different. The first time he met Gina, they'd been huddled at the same end of one of those long tables at the Middle East. He'd felt awkward and had blabbed on and on about the solo project he was working on—an opera about Anar-cho-Syndicalism, using feedback instead of voices. Most people laughed nervously when he ranted about this stuff, but Gina seemed to live in a world where this was perfectly ordinary, where everybody went home and composed op-eras on their four-tracks.

And besides, it was Gina who made the moves on him. They're standing over the jukebox, trying to pick out some songs, when she leans into him drunkenly. "Hey," she says. "I've got my own hotel room. You want to go there later?"

Walt feels his face flush. "Yeah," he says hoarsely. "I really do. But I mean, how? I can't just go back with you guys. How would I explain that?"

She makes a scrunched-up thinking face; she's amused,

he can tell, charmed by his confusion. "Just say you're going to hang out at the hotel with us for a while."

"But you don't know Hank and Lilly." Walt hears his
own voice crack. "They'll tease me. They'll be like, 'We
know what you're up to.'"

"You're so shy," she says, touching his hand.

He glances down at her. Her round face is turned up to
his, those black eyes with their long lashes. "Not with you,"
he says. But even so, he feels out of control, like all this is
happening on some other planet.

"Look," she says. "I'll take care of it. Let's leave right
now."

"Right now?" It hadn't occurred to him that they could
do that—ditch the others.

She's leading him back to the table. "Hey you guys," she
announces, "someone over there just told us about a party.
We're going to go try and crash."

Walt half expects them to make fun of the pathetic-ness
of this excuse, to say, "Sure, sure that's what you're doing."
But instead, they go along with it.

"Do you have Kelly's address, in case we don't meet up
again?" Lilly says, all concerned.

A few more good-byes, some discussion of logistics, and
then he and Gina are out on the street, hailing a cab. Inside
the car, she gives him a high five. "I can't believe we got
away. Man, I'm so sick of traveling in a pack."

He's speeding through a strange city with this woman he
hardly knows. And yet, he feels oddly at home. He credits

this to Gina—her skill at negotiating the awkward moments of seduction.

"You're really smooth," he says to her. "The way you got us out of there."

"Yeah, you think?" She moves closer, lifts his arm over her shoulder.

And then they're making out. Their faces fit together perfectly, and it seems that they're still talking, a new kind of conversation where tongues and lips communicate through touch. Then lying back with his head against the seat of the cab, he watches the dizzy swirl of lights out the window. He has to admit that part of Gina's sexiness is this world around her: cabs, a private hotel room, her face that he's seen on the video at his friend Kevin's house—and even the thought of Kevin floating just outside the cab window, peering in and saying, "Oh Jesus, that's Gina Jeffers you're with."

For seconds now and then, he actually feels like he's in a rock video, that there's some soundtrack going on behind them if he could only hear it. The rock-star thing: it's superficial, it's stupid, it's not even real, and yet he's suddenly realized what a grip it's always had on him.

"I'll get it," she says when the cab stops. And then, to the driver, "Can you give me a receipt?" She rolls her eyes at Walt. "For tax purposes."

"No way."

"Yes way," she says. "Our accountant says we have to." He feels a little pang of jealousy. He wants an accountant.

Up in her room, she flops down on the queen-sized bed. "I'm too drunk to waste energy on standing up," she says.

He walks around, taking in its stale smell and the sanitized-for-your-protection atmosphere. He glances over at her. She's lying with her arms over her head, knees up to her chest.

"What are you doing?" he says.

"My back exercises. This is very good for the sacrum."

He lies on the floor and folds his long legs on his chest in imitation of her.

"No, you've got to move your knees in a circular motion," she says.

For a while, they both rotate their knees, a comfortable silence between them.

"I love hotel rooms," he says.

"You just wait. You'll learn to hate them." She sits up.

He sits too, leaning against the bureau. Head rush. "Yeah, well, our band can't even afford motels usually. I haven't slept in a real bed for about a week."

"You can stay here if you want," she says.

He feels his face flush. "I didn't mean it that way. It wasn't some come-on."

"That's okay," she says. "I didn't take it that way. I'm always having friends stay in my room when I'm on tour. No big deal. You could sleep in your shirt." The bed thing seems to jog her mind. "Hey," she says, "didn't you used to be with Shazia Dohra? Why didn't she come out with us? I really wanted to meet her."

"Shaz is kind of antisocial. I think she's regretting that she ever agreed to go on tour. We may lose her soon."

"That's too bad. I was just wondering. I mean, it must be

hard, the whole ex thing. You guys sleeping in the same rooms and stuck in that van for ten hours a day."

"Yeah, it is hard sometimes," he says, thinking that's the end of it. But she wants to hear more. He considers what to tell her. For a minute, he has an urge to spill the whole stinking story. How he lived in San Francisco. How Shaz started coming over to his apartment to jam. How they slept together. How he knew that she had other lovers and didn't consider him a real boyfriend. How he moved east to grad school and she followed a few months later, and everything changed. How she lived in his group house with him. How she kept her shoes next to his in the closet, shared his tube of toothpaste, cut his hair the way she liked it. How he'd assumed this would go on and on. How easy he felt with her, coming in late from the lab to find her practicing her bass, the two of them conferring about little household matters. How she'd started going to dyke parties. How she met Kate. How she moved out. How the closet looked without her dainty, withered combat boots. How the room felt when he came home, everything exactly as he'd left it. How he assumed it had nothing to do with him because she was really gay. How, half a year later, they met for a drink and she showed up in a dress—he'd never seen her in a dress—and told him she'd fallen in love with a man. How he'd walked around all night, miles and miles, until the subway started running again in the morning. How his legs had shaken as he sat on the plastic molded seat. How he'd been washed over by the realization that Shaz failed to love him because he could not be loved. How he'd stared out at the sickly yellow lights in the gloom of dawn and wanted out of it, the world. How his housemate found him in bed, shivering and babbling, and took him to the emergency room. How he ended up in the bin.

He wants to tell Gina this, but it's not exactly first-date material. So instead, he says, "Shaz and I, we've been through a lot. At this point, we're like family. Actually, I'm kind of worried about her right now. She's way too obsessed with her immune system. She takes these herbal tonics three times a day."

"Tell me about it." Gina rolls her eyes. "Bandmates on weird diets. Phoebe's a vegan. She refuses to eat French fries from McDonald's because they're cooked in beef fat."

Walt tries to think of the next thing to say, and suddenly he can't. Behind her, the drapes hang in neat folds, like columns. On the shelf, the drinking glasses are lined up, wearing paper sheaves. And next to them, the ice bucket, with its reproachful presence. The hotel room is too perfect. It demands too much of him. Like he's supposed to stroll over to the minibar and say, "Will you have the Canadian Club or the Chivas Regal?" and then tweeze ice into two glasses with those tongs.

"I'm not good at this," he says in a small voice. "I haven't had sex with anyone for almost a year now."

Gina flops down on her stomach, looks right at him. "It's okay. I just like hanging out with you. Besides, I haven't been getting too much action myself. My boyfriend and I split up in June. Then I went through this period where I hated men."

Walt feels his eyes prickle, and he blinks several times. None of this is going to work out, he can feel it.

"What's the matter?" she says, but before he can answer she's up, turning the clock radio so she can see it. "Oh geez," she says. "I've got to be up in six hours to do this stupid interview. Look, I'm going to bed. Do you want to stay here?"

"Sure, okay." His voice comes out in a croak.

She disappears into the bathroom, comes out in a T-shirt and boxer shorts, brushing her teeth. He can see her breasts move under the loose fabric of her shirt. Her legs are muscular, thick at the knees.

He takes his turn in the bathroom. In the small, humming room, he suddenly realizes that he and Gina have been talking for hours. It's strange now to be alone. Thoughts keep swarming around in his head and he has the urge to run out and say them to Gina. Instead, he tries to compose himself, so he can make a halfway dignified reentrance into the room. He slaps some water on his face, rubs his teeth on a towel, takes out his contacts and uses some of her solution. Then he pulls off his jeans and sweater and lets his shirt fall over his underwear.

When he opens the door, she's turned the light off. "I'm sorry," she says, "I'm conking out. I set the alarm for eight. You can sleep through it if you want."

At that moment, he feels intimate with her, as if they've been married for years.

"Good night," he says, settling into place. And she's a stranger again. For a long time, he follows her breath, trying to tell if she's fallen asleep or is faking it. His palms are sweating; he's hunched up in a ball. The same thought keeps repeating in his head: if I don't make a move right now I'm hopeless. Then it's just that one word: now, now, now. Each time he thinks the word "now," he tries to make himself lunge toward her. Each time, he stays curled on his side of the bed.

When he wakes up in the middle of the night, his heart is pounding. For a moment, the room around him won't resolve itself into any place he knows. Then everything comes back into focus: the bedside table, the starched sheets, the warmth from the woman beside him.

He rolls to face her. She doesn't move. Finally he says, "Hey."

"Huh?" she says familiarly, as if she's used to someone talking to her when she's asleep.

"Were you awake?"

She turns to face him. "I was having these sexually frustrated dreams."

Then—with seemingly no in-between moment—they're grinding against each other. He's running his hand against the smooth length of her back, getting used to the feel of her. His first impression is that she's small and slippery, like a piece of soap. They yank their clothes off, squirming around to enjoy the bliss of bare bodies.

Leaving the lobby in the morning, he finds himself on a wide downtown street. People are scurrying along, feeding themselves in and out of buildings. He has no idea how to get back to Kelly's, but he's been touring so long that this doesn't particularly bother him. After a while the unfamiliar cities all melt into one place—a city without street names, inhabited by office workers on their breaks, Starbucks and Gaps in the downtown, and a McDonald's as you get out toward the highway. In this generic city, this franchise branch of America, you can be lost and not lost at the same time. You can be at home anywhere.

Waking up after a new lover is like that too. You're content to have all your bearings thrown off, to find yourself plopped down in any strange location. He keeps going over moments from the night before, savoring them: how he slept curled around Gina with one hand cupped over her belly, how she had tried to lick his eyeballs and then burst out laughing.

He wanders around for a while, thinking maybe he'll figure out the transit system and catch a bus back to Kelly's. But in the end, he calls her place and asks Hank to come pick him up.

"Sorry," Hank says, when he finally shows up. "I ended up on Lake Shore Drive going the wrong way. Hey, can you get out the map?"

Walt, sitting shotgun in the van, struggles with the glove compartment. He pulls out a brand-new Chicago map and unfolds it. Tomorrow it will join the pile under the back seat: New York City, stained with motor oil; Ohio, with ketchup on it; Michigan, balled up and torn.

Walt was afraid that Hank would tease him about getting laid, but Hank seems more concerned with navigation. "Can you read that street sign?" he says to Walt. "Where are we?" And for a while, they simply try to find their way back.

Finally, Hank glances over. "Hey, listen. I hope it went all right with Gina last night. We didn't ditch you, did we? I felt kind of guilty when we left that bar and went home without you."

"No, no. It was great," Walt says. "It was so incredibly great. I'm really falling for her. She's so incredible."

"Whoa, buddy," Hank says, glancing over. "You spent one night together. No need to start thinking up names for the kids yet."

"I just want it to work."

"Exactly. That's why you have to play it cool."

"You mean I should pretend I don't like her?"

Hank is silent a moment. "It's just . . . What if it were the other way around? What if she got really intense on you? Wouldn't you get scared off?" Hank pulls the van in front of Kelly's building and throws the engine into Park.

"No. I'd be relieved."

"Trust me, you'd pull back. It's human nature." They get out and Hank fishes in his pocket for Kelly's key and unlocks the door.

"Where is everyone?" Walt says.

"They went out to this place for brunch. We can go meet them if you want."

"No." Walt slumps into one of the chairs. "Let's stay here."

Hank lies on the sofa across from him. "I'm just saying," he begins again, "you're a good-looking guy. You're acting like Gina's the only one who will go out with you, but that's not true. I know at least three women who have crushes on you."

Walt's face gets hot. "You do? Come on, don't make fun of me."

"I mean it." Hank settles his feet up on the arm of the white couch. "That girl Candy? She does."

Walt remembers—she had a drink with them after one of the shows in Boston. Her skin looked too perfect, airbrushed almost, like she was a model or something. "Her? Give me a break."

"I'm not shitting you. After you left that night, she said you were cute."

"Why didn't you tell me?"

"I thought it was obvious, man, the way she was chatting you up. Look, I don't know what you're worried about— you could have five girlfriends if you wanted."

Walt shakes his head. "It's not like that. I can't be with just anybody." He glances away, feeling he's going to lose it. "Gina's so easy to talk to. We're on the same wavelength. And her body—it's so comfortable. I've never felt like this . . ."

Hank shakes his head. "Come on, get a grip. You're dissolving in a puddle all over the floor."

"I know," Walt says, squirming around in his chair. "I'd be a lot healthier if I were like you."

Hank curls around into a fetal position. "I don't know about that. Let's not think about that one. Anyway, where is Gina?"

"Getting interviewed by the *Tribune*."

"Really?" Hank stares at him, then sits up. "Oh, man. If we could only get press like that." He's silent for a moment, thinking. "You know, I really am happy for you, that you found Gina and all that. But if it doesn't work out—like if you guys were together for a while and then broke up . . ." Hank gazes at him thoughtfully.

"What?"

"She's kind of fed up with the Brood, isn't she?"

"I guess."

Hank says slowly, "Well, if she ever did become your ex, as far as I'm concerned, I'd grab her in a minute."

Walt feels the blood rush out of his face. "What?" He flashes on this picture of Hank grabbing Gina by the waist.

"Because let's face it," Hank is saying. "We're going to lose Shaz. If we had Gina, that would solve everything."

"Oh, for the band," Walt says. He hears how his own voice sounds—dead, emotionless. He gets up, stalks off to the other end of the loft.

"I'm sorry," Hank calls.

"Poor Kelly." Walt spits it out like an insult.

Hank trudges over, stands behind him. "What? Look, just forget what I said, okay?"

Walt turns around to face him. "You dumped Kelly. One day you decided it was a pain to have her around and you just got rid of her, didn't you? What I want to know is how you get away with stuff like that. I mean, she still worships you."

Hank is white. He seems smaller somehow, hunched into himself. "Hey, hey," he says. "Calm down."

Walt shakes his head. "Women always fall for guys like you. I mean, Kelly. You probably treated her like shit and she'll still do anything for you."

Hank's jaw tightens. "Would you stop with the Kelly stuff? You don't know what you're talking about." He breathes out a long puff of air, like he's trying to stay cool. "If you really want to know, Kelly had already decided to move to Chicago when I met her. I kept thinking she'd change her mind and stay. When she left, it really fucked me up."

"Uh-huh," Walt says. He's suddenly seen it, how Hank twists around the truth. How Hank always manages to get what he wants.

And now, a certainty has bloomed in his mind the way a bruise blooms on your skin with a dull, inevitable ache: He knows what will happen once the tour ends. Gina will take days to return Walt's phone calls; when they finally do see each other, she'll peck him on the cheek. And then one night she'll invite him out for a drink and explain why she can't be with him—she's on the rebound, or she met someone, or she wants to be alone, one of those reasons. Next thing, he'll walk into the practice room, and she and Hank will be hunched toward each other as they tune their bass and guitar together. She'll glance up at Walt furtively and then smile. "Oh, didn't you know?" she'll say. "I've been talking to Hank for a while. Now that I'm your ex, I can join the band. I hope you don't mind."

Now Walt takes a deep breath, trying to bring himself

back to the present, to the time before all that has happened. "You don't understand," he says. "This whole exes gimmick, I've always hated it. It's been awful for me."

"You never said anything."

"Well, maybe I should have." Walt hears his own voice getting loud. He hears himself saying things he didn't know. "The first year, I was still in love with Shaz, and I had to be around her all the time. Do you know what that's like? If I'd known how to take care of myself better, I wouldn't have joined this band. I mean, I'd just gotten out of the loony bin. Didn't you guys ever consider that? Being in this band could have sent me right back into McLean Hospital. Or did you only care about how I sounded on the drums?"

Hank glares at him. "I didn't know you then." He breathes in with a sharp, hissing sound. "Anyway, you could have quit if it was so horrible. You don't have any friggin' reason to complain. I'm the one who should complain. I do all the work." He shakes his head. "For two years, I've given up my life for this thing. I'm always the one who has to be the heavy. And you know, I hate acting like a jerk. But if I didn't kick everyone's ass, how do you think we would've gotten where we are?"

"Who cares where we are?"

"I do," Hank says quietly. "Like I said, you could quit anytime. Not me, though. I'm just some loser who never made it to college. This is the only thing I've got."

"Yeah, okay." Walt sighs. It's no use trying to make Hank understand, he sees that now. He's having this vision of the two of them stuck together like electrons orbiting the same nucleus, the two of them flying around together. But of course it's not just Hank and him. The whole band is like that, four people locked together by forces of attraction and repulsion.

You think of the atom as a solid thing, but it's not. Most of the space is taken up by the paths of maddened electrons, electrons moving so fast their exact location can never be determined. Walt's always felt sorry for those electrons—how they're tortured by their empty valences, buffeted around by their charges, trapped in their pointless orbitals. And now he's like that, too. He'd always thought of himself as an atom, but now he understands that he's really only an electron, a speck of something larger.

What happens in rock bands—the split-ups, the acrimony, the personnel changes—is only part of the painful dance of the universe. After all, each atom is a kind of molecular rock band: the elegant and stable helium would be the Beatles; oxygen would be a supergroup like Buffalo Springfield; and einsteinium—a fly-by-night, unstable atom—would be the Exes.

What is the fundamental law of nature? Things oscillate. Atoms do, bodies do, bands do. But Walt is fucking sick of oscillation. He wants out. He wants to give it a rest.

Seven hours later, he's carrying his drums onto the stage for the sound check. He glances out where the audience will stand and sees an endless cavern—yards of worn carpeting, a ceiling so high that it's lost in darkness, tiny bottles winking from the bar at the other end of the dance floor. His stomach drops. The place must hold a thousand people.

The club—the obscene hugeness of it—acts on all of them like a drug. Lilly's gone nuts. She's prancing around, pretending to be Mick Jagger or maybe one of the guys from Spinal Tap. "I'm not a pop musician," she keeps saying in a bad British accent. "I'm a philosopher."

Shaz is standing next to him, the neck of her bass bobbing whenever she turns, seeming to point at Walt like an accusing finger. "I don't want to do this," she says in a small voice. He feels almost like she's huddling toward him, wanting to crawl into his lap. In the last few days, things between them have turned upside down; now she's the one who stares at him hungrily, hoping for their old closeness.

He doesn't know how to answer her. "It'll be okay," he tries. "You're just getting the jitters."

"I'm worn out. Where am I going to get the energy to play to this kind of crowd?" And she does look exhausted— her face sagging in a way that's become familiar to him in the past few weeks.

"It's easy for you, remember?" he says.

Her stiff black hair hangs over her eyes and she doesn't bother to push it away. He notices how bitten-down her fingernails have become. "Why am I here?" she says. "Why aren't I home?"

A thunderous voice interrupts them. "Lead guitar," it says. He and Shaz both jump, looking around for the source of the noise.

"It's the sound guy," Walt says, shading his eyes against the lights and pointing to the faraway balcony, the white face somewhere out there in the gloom. The sound guy is speaking into his mike, his voice booming through the stacks of amps that sit on either side of the stage.

Hank plays a riff on his guitar. "Is that good?" he says into his mike, looking off toward the sound guy.

"Yeah," the voice says. It seems to issue from nowhere, or all around them, and yet it's oddly intimate. You can hear the smack of the guy's tongue on the top of his mouth, the ragged way he breathes. And Walt wonders how they got here, tiny figures on a stage, each playing a riff to the voice of God.

When it's Shaz's turn, she runs her fingers along the fret board of her bass, pursing her lips in concentration. Walt can tell she's terrified at the way every pop and slide of her fingers roars out of the Marshall stacks, echoing through the huge cave of this place.

"Okay, you guys are fine," the voice says. "Now I need the next band up here. Where's the Brood?"

No one knows. So Walt jumps from his stool and waves as he hurries off stage, as if to say, "I'll go look." He can't wait to get out of there.

He stumbles through the dark hallways backstage and down an ill-lit stairway that smells of damp concrete. He finds a door and has to grope around for the handle. When it finally opens with a peculiar kissing sound, he blinks in the sudden glare of the streetlights outside.

Right away, he sees the tour bus. It's the size of a Greyhound, with blacked-out windows and THE BROOD painted across the side in hot-pink letters. It's parked halfway up on the sidewalk in front of him, idling with a low thunder, its hazards blinking.

Some guy jogs down the stairs of the bus. He's got the hangdog look of a roadie, bald on top and wearing a grimy down jacket. "Hey," he says. "Prop that door open, will you? We kept banging on it, but nobody heard us."

Walt starts fooling with the door. While he's trying to get it to stay open, he hears the clatter of feet—more people coming off the bus. When he stands up again, Gina and David have appeared on the sidewalk. Huddled together, underdressed for the cold, they look like rock stars. Gina's short hair sticks out, like she's been sleeping on a floor and hasn't washed in days. Walt can't figure out how someone staying in hotel rooms can always appear to be so grimy.

She hurries over, colliding into him. "Hey," she says. "Want to go have a smoke with me?" A minute later, they're in the alley behind the building. She's got her cold nose pressed into his cheek, and he's feeling inside her mouth with his tongue, tentatively, as if to check that everything's still there.

"Sorry I left like that this morning," he says. "I didn't know if you wanted me to wait or not."

"I wish you hadn't split." There's urgency in her voice.

He stares into her huge pupils and then gently wipes the crumbly stuff, what they call the sleep, out of the corners of her eyes. Something between them shifts right then. He knows she will not melt away from him when they get back to Boston. He knows that she belongs to him.

"You're like a drug to me," he says. "The way your face looks and your smell and everything."

"Yeah," she says, her voice cracking. "You too."

They make out, huddling in the bitter wind. He gets his hands inside her shirt to feel the warm S of her back.

"We have to stay together tonight. We have to," she says urgently.

"I know."

"How are we going to pull it off? You guys are out of here early in the morning, right?" she says.

Before he can answer, there's a clunk, clunk, clunk of heavy boots on the pavement, and he glances up to see Phoebe with her arms crossed and her red hair blowing around her face.

"There you are," she says. "Gina, everyone's waiting."

Gina rolls her eyes at him and then jogs away. "See you later," she calls.

And Walt's left standing there in the alley, beside a Dumpster leaking some kind of goo that's frozen all over the asphalt. He stares up at the sky, past the streetlights, trying to see stars. But the sky is tissue-paper gray, as if a filmy scarf is hanging over the world. He has that feeling again, that elated sense of being unstuck, of being at home even in this alley with its tracks of ice shining on the ground, like cracks letting in light from whatever nether-world hides underneath.

Slowly, he walks around the sides of the club, trying

doors until one of them opens. He wanders around for a while, high from making out. In some corner backstage, he runs across Shaz. She's sitting on a musty couch, her head lolling. She smiles at him. He can't figure out why she's so happy.

"What's with you?" he says.

"There's a party." She's staring up at him, grinning.

"What kind of party would that be?" he asks. And he feels that old connection to her. They're in sync. They're flirting without intention. They're together but not—exes in a good way.

"Some party in the VIP room upstairs. It's really for the Brood, but I didn't know what else to do, so I went up there."

"Shaz," he says. "You hate things like that."

"I guess that's why I drank three vodka tonics." She laughs and is suddenly beautiful again, with her full cheeks and her dark eyes.

"I can't believe this. You're drinking?" This is about the last thing he would have guessed; these days, she only drinks wheatgrass shakes and herbal infusions, echinacia tea and carrot juice.

"I'm going to be an alcoholic for the rest of the tour. That's how everyone else deals with it, you know." She seems gleeful.

"You're kidding," he says. "I thought you didn't want to go on this tour for health reasons—you were afraid to, like, eat French fries and stuff."

She draws her knees up under her chin, settles in more

comfortably on the filthy sofa. "Oh, I'm sick of trying to control everything. I really shouldn't have come on this tour. But I'm here now, right?"

He puts his hands on his hips. "What happened at that party? Tell me."

Shaz rubs her face, tries to concentrate. "I went up to the room, and there's all these A&R guys standing around. One of them—I think he was from Geffen—shakes my hand and tells me I'm a genius."

"Oh, man."

"Yeah," she scrunches up her face. "I mean, I knew it was bullshit. Those guys tell everyone they're a genius. But, I don't know. The whole thing was too weird. I wanted to be holding something, you know? So I picked up this cup and took a few sips, and it was like, 'Yeah, this is exactly what I need.' I was just so glad for some alcohol at that moment."

"So what else did the guy say? What happened?"

"He wants me to play with some other band he's got." She shakes her head. "The guy tells me they're trying to 'package' this all-women band. I don't know what the fuck that means, but I'm pretending I understand. Then he says, 'We'd definitely have a place for you. I think you're the best woman bassist out there today.' Then he, like, leans toward me in this creepy way and says, 'The money would be incredible.'"

Walt's chest squeezes with some awful feeling. He realizes he's jealous. "That's great, Shaz."

"Don't let me do it, okay?" she pleads. "I'm such an idiot.

I know when something's wrong, but I always let myself get talked into it anyway."

"Why's it so wrong?" he says.

"Because they get you sucked in, and pretty soon you're miserable. The money never turns out to be what they promised." She sounds almost weepy now.

It's best to change the subject, he decides. "Hey, hear that? They've turned on the house sound." The floor is vibrating under his feet with the dull thud of club music. "Come on, let's go see."

They climb some stairs to the balcony and lean over a railing, watching as people flood in. And then time speeds up. Or rather, everything else goes into fast-forward while he and Shaz seem to move in slo-mo. He tries to convince her to go back down the stairs, but she doesn't want to leave the balcony. Then they get lost wandering around backstage. He keeps having to say, "Come on, Shaz, or I'm going to leave you," because she wants to sit down on the floor.

They're about a half-hour late getting to the dressing room, and he expects someone to be pissed. But no one seems to have noticed they were missing. Lilly's in a frenzy. "Where's my spare set of strings?" she's yelling. Hank's leaning up against the wall with his eyes closed.

Walt taps him on the shoulder.

Hank opens his eyes, but stares straight ahead. "They want us to go on soon. I mean, whenever we're ready." He sounds like a zombie.

"I don't want to," Shaz says.

Lilly grabs to her arm. "Me neither."

And then something takes hold of Walt. "Okay," he says, "let's go." And without waiting for the rest of them, he walks out onto the stage. He hears the crowd clap and yell; he can sense them out there, moving toward the stage, massing.

He sits down on his stool. In the harsh light, he notices every scratch and stain on the skins. He can smell his own sweat and the mildewy basement stink of the towel inside the bass drum. The other three fall into place around him. It's the same feeling as when you're a kid and your family piles into the car, everyone knowing which seat to take.

Walt nods at the sound man, and the canned music snaps off. In the sudden silence, he hits his sticks together four times, and then they all fall on their instruments at the same time, launching into "Tilt." The song goes by in a blip; it barely lasts a second. Walt glances down at the play list that Lilly has taped on the floor for him, the names of the songs in her loopy scrawl. "Gore." "Evil Can Evil." "Hot Dog." "Gator." The songs pass as fast as subway trains. He's watching his arms fly around him; they move with their own intelligence, whirling like helicopter wings.

And then, he gets to the place on the list where Lilly has written "break for intros." He stops, puts his sticks across the snare drum. His chest is wet with sweat. Lilly's out there in the light, dancing around in front of her mike, talking in that exaggerated Southern drawl. She's pulling her dress across her belly so they can see the swell. He watches her dreadlocks bob, the sweat shine on the back of her neck. And then she's introducing Hank, and he's soloing on his guitar, slapping the effects boxes with his foot so the thing sings. And then Lilly announces her own name and picks out a rockabilly boogie on her guitar. Next it's Shaz, with a walking bass line.

Then Lilly calls his own name. On cue, he flies into a solo, his drums talking in patterns of logic he's overheard in the loony bin and glimpsed through the microscope, an argument that comes together in crescendos like words that make almost perfect sense. And for a moment, he knows why he's been put here under the hot press of lights with the neuron net of electric cords snaking around him. To understand that he shouldn't be alone, not even inside his own head. To hear how his drums sound raw and naked without the other instruments. To understand that this thing he calls himself—this nattering voice that never stops, this consciousness, this drum solo—is part of something larger.

Walt settles back into a simple beat. He's got his elbows down at his sides now, wrists flicking out the rhythm. They're watching him—Hank, Lilly, and Shaz. He perceives them in pieces: Hank's fingers curled around his pick, Lilly's ecstatic O of a mouth, Shaz's foot hovering over the pedal of her flanger. They're ready. They're waiting for a signal from him. He's the drummer, the one who shows them when to stop and start, the one who decides how fast to go, the one who carries them along on his beat and in his van, the one who can make them erupt into sound with one nod of his head. He nods.